MR CAMPION'S FALCON

Matthew James Matthews dies of natural causes whilst staying at the upmarket Drover's Arms in the Cotswolds. Max Newgate, the pompous manager of the inn, is found dead miles away in a Suffolk river near an archaeological dig. The star geologist of Omega Oils, the brilliant but eccentric Francis Makepeace, could be connected to both, but he has disappeared and seems determined not to be found. It takes all Campion's guile and charm to get to the bottom of the mystery and ensure that the new, youthful allies he recruits emerge unscathed.

MR CAMPION'S FALCON

MR CAMPION'S FALCON

by

Youngman Carter

Magna Large Print Books
Long Preston, North Yorkshire,
BD23 4ND, England.

British Library Cataloguing in Publication Data.

Carter, Youngman
    Mr Campion's falcon.

    A catalogue record of this book is
    available from the British Library

    ISBN   978-0-7505-3956-2

First published in Great Britain in 1970

Copyright © Trustees of the Margery Allingham Society, 2013

Cover illustration by arrangement with Ostara Publishing

The moral right of the author has been asserted

Published in Large Print 2014 by arrangement with
Ostara Publishing

Magna Large Print is an imprint of Library Magna Books Ltd.

Printed and bound in Great Britain by
T.J. (International) Ltd., Cornwall, PL28 8RW

I am grateful to Mr Monja Danischewsky for the use of his profound knowledge of certain byways in the Cotswolds, and I regret that one village in particular, though familiar to many of us, cannot be found on a map. Apart from this, no reference is intended to any existing place, company or individual, nor to any recent discovery, whether archaeological, geological, geographical or gastronomic.

1

Miss Peregrine's Progress

Mr Max, whose staff called him 'His Excellency' behind his back, had not been given the title out of affection.

For his guests at the Drover's Arms, the four-star country hostelry which epitomized Old England in the eyes of wealthy tourists, he was a host so smooth and efficient that nothing of his personality remained in their memory the moment their needs were satisfied.

To that extent he had ambassadorial quality, but there were other less obvious ingredients behind the façade and the dominant of these was curiosity. It was the mainspring which kept every cog moving. An unsolved problem, whether it was the extramural activities of a week-end party, the theft of a pepper-pot or the identity of an unlikely visitor, brought him an exquisite discomfort. The riddle which obsessed him at the moment was near to torture.

His office, an unpretentious modern cubicle behind the reception desk, was equipped with a two-way mirror through which he could observe the hub of his world whilst remaining invisible.

The arc of vision included the oak staircase with its mercifully shallow treads, the doors to the Coffee Room, the Ostler's Bar and the Refectory, the service corridor, a long table gay with international magazines for ever pristine, a landscape attributed to Constable, a set of coloured stipple prints by Morland and, most important of all, the entrance.

He was watching this now, a sleek black cat in pin-stripe trousers, totally absorbed in his private mystery.

Presently a girl would come through the bright rectangle, a little piece of the jigsaw to be twisted and memorized until he found where it fitted.

The minutes, articulated by an octagonal coaching clock facing the reception desk, dragged on, heightening the tension, and his reflexes twitched, forcing him to shift his weight from a leg which was suddenly numb.

Half-past three. Later than he had calculated.

He was not the only watcher. In the far corner beside the bow window beyond his line of vision a man in flagging grey mohair, gross as a laughing buddha, was concealing his face behind a newspaper. When the barrier was lowered a pair of tinted glasses gave the impression that the owner might be nearly blind, but the eyes, bolstered in flabby fat, were shrewd enough.

The August sun patterned the floor with squares of gold, turning each new arrival into a silhouette, so that Mr Max had to wait until the girl paused half-way to the desk before he was absolutely certain. She was not quite as he had pictured, but there could be no mistake.

She was carrying a small overnight case, and her black moiré silk tailor-made coat was two years out of date. Borrowed, he decided, but originally from the boutique of a good house. She was not wealthy, then, but the background was promising.

Nineteen? Twenty-three? It was impossible to guess. Attractive to a man with enough courage: probably intelligent. He added the final item to the debit side with regret.

He glided to the counter, cutting off the official receptionist on his way, and reached it precisely as the girl pulled off a bright orange bandanna scarf and shook out the unfashionably short chestnut curls on the top of her head.

'My name is Peregrine,' she said. 'You rang me. I came as quickly as I could.'

Mr Max flexed his lips. It was not a smile but a formality conveying recognition and impersonal welcome.

'Of course. About Mr Matthews. It was very sudden – very unfortunate. The staff and

13

I would like to offer you our sincere regrets. We were all extremely distressed – shocked, if I may say so. I have reserved a room for two nights, or for longer should you wish. If you would care to see it…'

To her eyes he seemed nearer an automaton than a man. His body, if flesh and blood existed below the shining collar and dove-grey tie, had been designed to fit the jacket and the oval face with its peak of straight hair had less reality than a tailor's dummy. The voice, classless and apparently pre-recorded, flowed on.

'…a very pleasant outlook over the garden. The Chaucer Room. Mr Matthews always reserved the Milton suite, but we thought you might prefer something smaller.'

He paused for her agreement and produced a sheet of hotel notepaper from a folio.

'In case it is of service I have prepared a short list of people you may wish to contact. The Coroner's Office, for example.'

A slim gold pen indicated the name.

'Do I have to see him?' said Miss Peregrine. 'I thought a doctor had been attending Mr Matthews?'

It was not going to be quite as easy as Mr Max had supposed. The girl was completely controlled, as unemotional as any other overnight guest. The fact that she was attractive might mean offers of help from the most unlikely quarters. He had hoped for a

14

suppressed tear, a chink through which he could pry into her thoughts. He was still deferential but a trace of authority crept into his voice.

'I'm afraid so. Any sudden death is a matter for the Coroner. In this case Dr Penn, who had advised Mr Matthews occasionally, was away and his deputy apparently could not find the case history. The question, as I expect you know, has now been satisfactorily answered. There will be no inquest, no difficulties of that sort.

'The officer – his name is Leatherdale by the way – removed some personal possessions from Mr Matthews's room, a briefcase and so on. Proof of identity. No doubt, if you are going to assume other responsibilities you will wish to recover them?'

He raised his eyes without moving his head.

'I hope you *are* going to take charge? You see, we know of no other friends or relations and we would be glad to leave everything in your hands if it is at all possible.'

'Oh yes,' said Miss Peregrine. 'I'm taking charge.'

'I'm extremely relieved. Mr Matthews was one of our very regular guests. My staff were happy to serve him and in a way you could say that he made his home here. One would not like to think of him without a friend at such a time.'

Again the pencil moved delicately over the page.

'I have added the name of the undertaker who has made all the necessary arrangements. In case you don't know our little town – it is really no more than a village street full of antique shops – I shall be glad to direct you.

'Dr Penn, who is back now, lives almost next door. He's been most helpful. Mr Russell, of Russell and Clarke, is our only solicitor, but no doubt you have your own. The Vicar is Mr Telkamp. I understand Mr Matthews was Church of England.'

'I – I think so. Does it matter?'

Her hesitation might be a sign of weakness. He glanced as high as her chin, but it revealed nothing.

'Probably not, madam. No doubt the Vicar agrees with you, for the funeral is arranged for three o'clock tomorrow. The florist on your list is Miss Margrave, just at the foot of the hill. If there is anything else...?'

She shook her head.

'You seem to have thought of everything.'

For the first time he was unable to keep his voice as impersonal as he wished.

'You knew the late Mr Matthews very well?'

'Oh yes. He was going to live at Brett quite near the school in a house which belonged to me. I was furnishing it for him and he was coming to stay with us until the place was ready. I suppose you found my address on the heavy luggage? Some of it has already arrived.'

Mr Max risked a smile which was meant to be engaging.

'Your name has been known to me for some time, Miss Peregrine. Mr Matthews gave it to me for forwarding his mail on several occasions – in fact it is the only address we have on our files. I felt I was justified in getting in touch with you when the tragedy occurred. The police, that is, the Coroner's officer, advised that I should do so. There seemed to be no one else to whom I could mention the matter.'

'It was very thoughtful of you. They rang me just before you called. They didn't seem to know a great deal, so perhaps you can tell me what really happened.'

Deliberately, he lowered his voice to a murmur, so that she had to bend towards him.

'We found Mr Matthews, asleep, as the maid thought, at about half-past ten in the morning. This was on Wednesday, the day before yesterday. He was an early riser by habit – a seven-thirty call – but it was some time before we realized he had passed away. I called Dr Penn, but it was the young man, Dr Lee, the new junior partner, who arrived, though there was nothing to be done. Dr Penn when he returned yesterday was able to prevent any unpleasantness. He had treated Mr Matthews for a heart condition I believe. He was quite satisfied about the cause of death – in fact, he told me he had been expecting it.

'The question which arose, among others of course, was about Mr Matthews's effects: his car for example is still garaged here. As a hotelier – an innkeeper is the legal term – I have certain responsibilities to my guests. You see, although he was no stranger to us at the Drover we really know nothing of his background so to speak. He arrived on Monday, intending to stay for three nights. He kept an account at the bank here, but Mr Morgan the manager – his name is on your list – knows as little as I do. Naturally I never inquired until this tragic occurrence. I assumed, if you'll forgive me, that he had recently retired ... an engineer, perhaps? He seemed a very practical gentleman?'

'An archaeologist,' said Miss Peregrine. 'At least, that was his main interest.' She picked up the typescript. 'Well now, you've really been very useful. Just have my case sent up. I'm sure the room will be splendid. Just for tonight, please. I'll try to see as many of these people as possible this afternoon.'

He looked after her retreating back with such intensity that the glowing space of the doorway made his eyes dazzle. So far he had learned precisely as much as Miss Peregrine had intended, which was as tantalizing as an itch in an inaccessible spot. She had not even signed the register. He carried the overnight case up to the Chaucer Room himself, placed it at the foot of the half-tester bed and eyed it speculatively. It was, he discovered, locked.

The single street of Great Burdon, called in the guide-books 'a jewel in the diadem of the Cotswolds', was very much as Mr Max had described it. From the T-junction of roads where the Drover stands beside a small green it runs gently downhill to the bridge and the church, veers left and climbs again to the edge of Burdon Woods. Behind the golden ochre of Cotswold stone, the best of English domestic architecture from Tudor to Georgian, every other window displays antiques at inflated prices and visitors touring between Oxford and the Shakespeare country fall easy victims to the expertise of salesmen twice armed with guile and charm.

In high summer after the last customer in the Drover's panelled refectory has paid his luncheon bill and the world seems kindly, sales resistance is low and trade is excellent.

Judged by results, Miss Peregrine had a satisfactory afternoon. Dr Penn, a deliberate and cautious Scot, unbent more easily than was his habit. He angled delicately to discover the precise relationship between the girl and his patient and decided that it was irreproachable.

'Of course I'd only known him for a short time – two years,' she explained frankly. 'We had interests in common – archaeology, and so on. He stayed with us – my father and myself – several times, and he should have come down yesterday to make final arrangements for moving to Brett. I think it was my cottage that really attracted him. Mother left it to me and I've been trying to let it for some time. I look after my father who's a housemaster at the School. It's a nice cottage, rather remote but very convenient for the ship.'

'An amateur sailor man, was he now? He did not tell me that.'

'The ship,' said Miss Peregrine, 'is Roman. You may not have heard of it, though some of the papers wrote about it. It was discovered two years ago at the edge of the playing-fields where the Brett river used to run before it changed course. The digging is still going on. It's late Roman, fourth century A.D., Carthaginian in design they say, about one hundred feet long and probably carried quite a lot of cargo. The mud seems to have preserved it because it dried out quite soon after the ship sank. Very exciting. Mr Matthews was coming down to help.'

Dr Penn sighed.

'The poor man. He missed his treat which is sad. He'd been a great worker in his day and his body was tired. I told him he'd have to be easy with himself. I hadn't the heart to go further and nor had he, as it fell out.'

He considered her cannily from beneath shaggy brows, hesitated on the verge of a question and changed his mind.

'I'm glad he's got a friend to put his affairs in order. You'll find its a thankless task, but that's the way of things. He has no relatives you are aware of? No business associates?'

'He'd lived abroad most of his life, I think. He never mentioned a family and the police – the coroner, that is – obviously couldn't discover any. That's why they phoned me.'

'Very sensible. Leatherdale – you'd best see him as soon as you can – is an intelligent fellow but not over-fond of work. He'll be relieved to see you, I don't doubt.'

Miss Peregrine's progress continued.

Before she returned to the Drover's Arms she had seen every name on Mr Max's list with the exception of the bank manager, and with P.C. Leatherdale she had scored an instant success. Over the years he had developed a technique which earned him the indulgence of his superiors and the gratitude of those unhappy members of the public with whom he had to deal. He was a tea-and-sympathy man, full of tactful advice which flowed easily from a store of suitable clichés which never dried. When there was work to be done the relatives and friends of the deceased were glad to leap to the assistance of this warm-hearted soul. He did remarkably well out of it, reaping a private harvest of pipes, pullovers and whisky every Christmas.

Miss Peregrine struck him as a natural – educated, trustworthy and unlikely to cause trouble. He approved of beauty if the possessor seemed unaware of the quality. He unloaded a briefcase containing business documents which were remarkably uninformative, and a faded passport some years out of date issued by the British Consul in an African state which had ceased to exist, showing that Matthew James Matthews had been born in Delhi in 1902, a British subject, six feet one with grey eyes and brown hair. With the case went an envelope containing a wristwatch, a pen, a cheque-book, a driving licence, reading glasses, a bunch of keys and a wallet holding £27 in notes.

'The smallest of the keys,' said Constable Leatherdale, 'opens the poor gentleman's brief-case. Just check the items through and I'll get you to sign for them. Another cup of tea?' He leaned forward confidentially.

'You know, miss, I always feel ashamed at meddling in other people's business especially at a time like this. You're a very young woman and it does my heart good to see the way you're coping with a sad loss. A much-respected gentleman he was, they tell me at the Drover. Just your signature and address, miss, and I won't trouble you any more.'

'You're very kind,' said Miss Peregrine, and signed her name in a trim round hand.

He watched her moving briskly down the street towards Miss Margrave of the Cotswold Nosegay Boudoir, approving her self-possession. 'Neat,' he said to himself. 'Neat but not too flash. You don't often see them like that these days. No trouble there.'

A particular question had been on his lips more than once during the interview but like Dr Penn he had suppressed it. It was probably of no importance.

The Drover's Arms expected its guests to dine late and to take their time about it. The food ranged from what was coyly described as 'The Farmer's Ordinary', a steak and kidney pie enriched with bacon, oysters, pigeons and tinned quails' eggs, to *Caneton à l'estragon* preceded by *Filets de Sole Beaumanière*. Miss Peregrine took an omelette, some cold roast beef and a piece of Stilton, thereby earning the head waiter's open approval. Attractive women, in his experience, often had horrible taste in food.

Mr Max hovered in his best diplomatic manner, finally sending over a half bottle of Corton with his compliments. He had given instructions that she should be placed at the best of the small tables where he could keep an eye on her.

She was wearing a russet dress of wool gaberdine, very simply cut, which set off the rich brown of her hair and brought a glow to the amber beads at her neck. 'Quite a dish,' said the head waiter surveying his crowded kingdom as he paused for a moment beside the sommelier. 'I wonder what His Excellency is up to. She's a friend of old Matthews, the one who died in Milton. H.E.'s after something and I wouldn't say it was a date.' His elderly colleague considered the problem. 'Mr Max Bloody Newgate never does anything without a reason. There's something in it for him — or he thinks there is.'

It was a warm night. The mullion windows of the Refectory gave on to a terrace set with white wrought-iron tables and evergreens in square tubs. The interesting guest having finished her meal took herself, and her book, to this typical old English arbour. The coffee was better than she had expected and she read for some time before the creak of a chair on the other side of the table made her look up sharply. She did not like what she saw.

In the curious mixture of lighting, the one half coming from warmly shaded lamps and the other from a full moon, the man opposite her looked as if he had been unkindly moulded from a mass of builder's putty. He was bald save for a wisp of black hair over the dome of his forehead running from ear to ear. A reflection of light made his eyes invisible behind pale blue-green lenses.

'Miss Anthea Peregrine? Forgive me for joining you. If I am intruding ... but of course I am intruding, and by intention ... you will have to leave me, for I am incapable of moving myself any further. I am intruding, then, but for an excellent reason. May I have some conversation with you?'

The voice was thick and husky, suggesting an asthmatic or a brandy drinker, the tone unconvincingly servile.

Miss Peregrine met his blank glasses levelly for some time before she placed a marker in her book and closed it.

'I've had a very long day and I'm thinking of going to bed.'

'My name is Porteous,' he said, 'Claude Porteous.'

'Should I know you?'

Words tumbled from his mouth in a wheezy rumble which was only broken when he paused for breath.

'I am a stranger to you, as you observe. Any man as gross, as grotesque as I am, is memorable, so you have certainly never seen me before. You may think me impertinent – I am impertinent – I have great temerity. But not without reason. I hope you will see eye to eye with me on this when I explain. May I continue? It really is in your best interest that you allow me to continue.'

'Go on then.'

'You are very civil. Perhaps civilized is a

better word. I would have expected no less from a friend of Mr Matthews. A civilized avuncular relationship is what I anticipated. I understand that you are watching over his affairs – that you are relieving the police, the hotel, the lawyers, the public trustee and so on, of a lot of tedious responsibility. That is very kind – true proof of friendship. It would make my position much easier if you would confirm this suggestion. It would justify my intrusion. Do you accept that?'

'Did you know Mr Matthews?'

The fat man sighed.

'Unfortunately we had never met. I came here, so to speak, to observe him, a little matter which I had to leave uncompleted. I am not a mobile person – my bulk makes exertion very dangerous to me – but I have other eyes and ears. Such items are available – they are for hire.

'Tell me, Miss Peregrine, apart from yourself and presumably your circle, do you know of any friend or associate of Mr Matthews in all the world?'

She shook her head.

'Then I am in order if I address my inquiries to you?'

'It depends what you want to know. If it's business you'd better write to my solicitors. I've asked them to...'

He interrupted her by tapping the table lightly with his fingers.

'I don't think it will wait, young lady. This afternoon you went to the Police Station and collected a brief-case among other items belonging to your friend. I will not speculate about the contents and I very much doubt if you would enlighten me if I inquired. But I ask you to show me the case itself. Empty the contents by all means – they probably mean as little to you as they would to me. But I wish to examine the object itself – to satisfy my curiosity if you like. Will you bring it to me?'

'Why on earth should I do that?'

A movement of his head had made his eyes visible in a long unwavering stare which did not match the whine of his voice. His breathing was shallow, moving the pouches round his jaw as if he were a contemplative toad.

'Because it could be to your advantage. You have nothing to lose, perhaps a great deal to gain.'

He leaned forward. 'You are a very self-assured young woman – of course you are at your age and it is admirable, wholly admirable – but even you have your share of curiosity. I can show you something which may open your eyes. *Run along now.*'

The final words were a challenge if not an order. He turned away from her, easing his bulk farther into his chair so that it creaked again. A minute passed before the girl showed any sign of reaction. Then she straightened her back and left the terrace but he made no sign that he had noticed her departure.

Nor did he acknowledge her return. His head remained bowed, his hands clasped over a heavy walking-stick upright between his legs. For a moment she wondered if he were asleep and she moved her coffee cup sharply, making it rattle before she placed the brief-case on the table.

'Well?'

It was an elaborate case made of thick pigskin, a brown version of the type used by government officials with a businesslike lock and the initials M.J.M. in gold mounted at one corner. He turned slowly, rested the stick on the bench beside her and lifted the case a couple of inches, testing its weight.

'You have kept this locked?'

'Of course. It is open now.'

'And it is empty now. Very sensible of you. You suspect me of prying into your affairs – I *am* prying into your affairs – and you very naturally resent my behaviour. Yet you have an inquiring mind. I have excited your curiosity – I had no other weapon – but now I hope to gratify you.'

He spread out the base of the brief-case until it opened like an old-fashioned camera and stood it upright on the table, an impressive symbol of executive status.

'This is a design much used by smugglers until a couple of years ago. Now it is suspect – an encumbrance, an embarrassment for honest travellers because it invites suspicion. The secret has been discovered – circulated to every Customs officer in the land. I am not suggesting your departed friend used this device for anything but the most prudent of purposes – the protection, the concealment of valuables.'

His glasses had become dark convex mirrors again, reflecting her own silhouette and the windows behind her. He broke off to recover his breath and spoke abruptly.

'You have not discovered this trick? My time is more valuable than yours. I am not here to waste it.'

Miss Peregrine shook her head.

'Very good. Then I will teach you the secret. Put the case on its side, the lock downwards and the handle towards me – so. Now on the underside you will see a small row of studs, part of the binding, you might suppose – you are meant to suppose. There are five of them, or should be. Am I right?'

'Quite right.'

'Then press the ones at each end as hard as you can. They should make a little click when the force is sufficient. And now the centre stud. Press very hard indeed with your thumb and twist it a trifle anti-clockwise.'

'A false bottom,' she said. 'Very ingenious.'

She had opened a narrow strip, the top of a hidden pocket at the side of the case, and was exploring the cavity with a small sunburnt hand.

'Should there be anything in it?'

If he was surprised or angry the glasses concealed the emotion.

'Certainly.'

She pushed her wrist deep into the recess, feeling every corner. Finally she lifted the case and shook it thoroughly.

'It's quite empty. Look for yourself.'

The fat man picked up his stick and rested his hands on the ivory crook.

'Then you have been robbed, Miss Peregrine – that is, assuming that you have charge of your friend's property. A considerable sum.'

'How do you know? I thought you said you never met Mr Matthews?'

'So I did. But I also said I had eyes and ears at my disposal. On Tuesday night our friend placed twelve hundred and fifty pounds in that cavity. The sum is large but the space it occupies in £10 notes is surprisingly small – a stout envelope, no more. On Wednesday morning he was dead, a natural death – that is beyond question. I think you can rule out police or the hotel employees as thieves. They lack both the information and the temerity. The case has been lying unattended in your bedroom for some two hours, but the key is no doubt in your handbag and the pocket cannot be opened when the case is locked. The mechanism is delicate and there has been no forcing. It makes the position very interesting.'

He paused for breath, wheezing audibly and raised a single finger to prevent her speaking.

'You will ask two questions, no doubt. Two questions are essential. The first is: can you believe a word I say? As to that you will please yourself but I have not imposed on you without reason. The second is: if you credit your loss, what can you do about it? I can offer you advice on this point, though there is no reason why you should take it. If you are wise you will do nothing at all.'

The girl had made no social concession to the meeting. She sat very still and formal, returning the blank stare without flinching.

'And suppose I ignore your advice?'

'If you do that, my dear young lady, you will be making an ass of yourself and causing a lot of unnecessary trouble. Consider your position. The money, if it existed – and there is only my word for it – is not yours. My word is ephemeral, and if pressed I shall deny having given it. There is no possible proof that anything I have told you is true. I am leaving this hotel tonight and it is conceivable that you will never see me again. I came to extract information from you and you have told me all I wish to know. You seem to me quite capable of looking after yourself and you should take some precautions to that end.'

He stood up. It was a slow process involving the placing of much of his weight on the stick.

'There is one other question. If it has been asked before during your calls of this afternoon you must forgive me.'

'I may not answer it.'

'Very possibly not. But it could put a thought in your head. Did you know that the late Mr Matthews wore a wig?'

2

Vanishing Trick

The two men who had reached the ritual stage of coffee and brandy after dinner at Fitzherberts, the oldest club in St James's Street, regarded each other with only qualified approval although they were old friends. Mr Albert Campion saw in his companion, L.C. Corkran, a man who was becoming too much like his surroundings; both were impeccable, chilly and a trifle out of date. As head of an obscure government department known unofficially as Security he had reached pensionable age, received the customary honour on retirement and had established himself in bachelor comfort in a house overlooking the Sussex Downs.

He was dapper in a soldierly fashion with trim white hair and a face which missed being handsome or impressive through a suggestion that pedantry was the weakness which had denied him martial success. Irreverently his friends called him Elsie.

Corkran for his part regarded Campion as a dilettante whose flashes of brilliance were irritatingly concealed behind a façade of vagueness, a deliberate air of anonymity encouraged by oversize horn-rimmed glasses which gave him the expression of an affable if sleepy owl. At sixty he was still slim and athletic, still deceptively vague.

Both men knew each other too well to be influenced by their defensive screens.

His host, Campion reflected, did very little without motive and at the chosen moment, after the cigars were satisfactorily alight and the cognac was mellowing the mind, the opening move would be made.

It was a situation which both men understood perfectly, each savouring the preliminary moves from an individual standpoint.

'My retirement,' said Corkran at long last, 'has been greatly exaggerated. Did you know that?'

The thin man was sufficiently surprised to blink. His host had never been particularly popular in the ivory towers of government and his tacit contempt for ministers regardless of public party or private opinion had earned him respect rather than appreciation. The idea that he might have been recalled seemed improbable and Campion said so. Corkran exhaled a cloud of smoke, fanning it contemptuously into the distance.

'An unlikely supposition. I was never political and our present masters are very political animals though they qualify as *homo sapiens*, one supposes. No, there has been nothing in the nature of a return. What I have done is to scramble from one pool, like an experienced crab, into a more promising one next door.'

Mr Campion enjoyed the analogy though he found the self-analysis uncharacteristic. The explanation would emerge in good time.

'You've moved into industry?'

'Precisely. My new overlord is Omega Oils, so you could say that I have exchanged national security for the international variety. The problems are very much the same but the scale is even larger. Certainly the rewards are more satisfactory. Omega stretches from London to Peru and New York to Xanadu, under several hundred company titles. All that you know of them is the top of the iceberg. Their predators are the rich relations of those I've always dealt with but more ruthless because they are better paid and therefore better organized.'

He took a sip of cognac and rubbed his nose. 'Patriots, zealots, political theorists and all the smaller fry I've been used to handling were generally an inefficient lot, thank God – often carrying a load of chips on their shoulders which one could scarcely miss. The best of them had blind spots engendered by devotion to some personal cause. My new customers are very different. Cash is the driving force and it buys international brains, unemotional craftmanship, expensive

35

equipment. It's a new world, Albert – new to me, that is. I find it fascinating.'

'Computerized?'

Corkran snorted. 'You could say that and it is true up to a point. But the human element remains. A brilliant man known for his austerity can still fall for a cocotte and betray his whole way of life and the cocotte may turn out to be just a home-loving girl after all. It's rare – and platitudinous – but I've known it to occur. The machine doesn't really run to psychology however hard it tries because it can never possess all the data.

'This organization of mine – my predecessor died very opportunely – has experts chosen by machines, analysed by machines, indoctrinated by machines, checked and cross-checked, tabulated, card-indexed. And yet if one piece of grit – like a concealed influence or an unrecorded vanity – gets into the works, the whole effort is wasted.'

'Where do you come in? As the old-fashioned watchdog with a genuine unmechanized bark?'

'I come in,' said Corkran primly, 'at the top. And on my own terms. Industrial espionage is understood and can be dealt with on every plane except the Board Room, which is what was called Cabinet level in my last sphere. I have an office which is cleaned by some form of automation and is so protected that no one but myself and my secretary is ever alone

36

there, and an appointment which is covered by a form of words which only three people understand. Security is genuinely respected. I can spend a fortune without question, which makes an exceedingly pleasant change, and I can employ any man or methods I please.'

'And you have a problem?'

Mr Campion's mild tone did not conceal his amusement. On the last occasion when they had met the position had been reversed and Corkran had exhibited that side of his personality which had earned him the reputation of behaving like an Olympian don. He was acutely aware of the reversal and disliked it. As a concession and an admission he ordered a second brandy.

'Have you heard of Francis Makepeace?'

'Never.'

Corkran raised one silver eyebrow and contracted the other in a frown.

'An eminent figure in his own world, which is probably remote from yours. A geologist. I have a file on him which is longer than most novels. He has worked in Omega for the best part of his life, and probably knows more about the location of oil in the world than any man living. Until four years ago he was our senior adviser, but his behaviour for some time before that had been erratic – so much so that he came under my predecessor's attention. When he was due to retire, he commuted his pension for a considerable sum which we cannot trace and that probably means a Swiss bank account. Some form of legal tax evasion would be characteristic – understandable in his case. Since then he has continued to work for us for a series of separate fees, plus a retainer. An odd, opinionated personality by any estimate – admired and disliked in equal proportion, but held in respect by every contact. Mental development arrested, I would say at the age of twenty-three. He resents growing old and likes to work in the field – an adventurer, you would call him. In some ways an undergraduate mentality. "The Boy Francis" was his nickname for many years and it appears to fit. Certainly he hates red tape or office discipline. Reading the dossier I found myself very strongly attracted, for his minutes make excellent entertainment. Some of them I might have written myself.'

'And now?'

'And now he has elected to vanish.'

'He must have done it extremely efficiently to escape your net.'

Corkran twirled the brandy in his glass and scowled at the golden liquid.

'As you say. Extremely efficiently. He is an efficient man and an energetic one. Whatever he has done he must have planned for a long time. His flat is closed and virtually empty of everything personal. His only other addresses are his bankers in Pall Mall and his club, the Travellers' of course, is in the same street. The routine men in my organization have come up with nothing and knowing the sort of fellow he is I would believe he legislated for their efforts in advance. This was very carefully done. A piece of negative evidence substantiates the theory. There is no photograph of Makepeace in the file, despite the fact that this is a breach of the rules. We know his blood group, his medical history and we have his fingerprints, his height, his weight, even a tape recording of his voice. But no photograph, except for one taken thirty-odd years ago which is, they tell me, unrecognizable. It argues intention over a period. And some degree of deceit. In my last job one of the simple methods of identifying an agent was to find the man who consistently avoided being present when everyone else was in the group picture. I'm afraid it makes the whole business suspicious and unsavoury.'

The guest considered the story during an extended pause. At this late hour the club was almost deserted and smoke hung in the air undisturbed.

'It occurs to me,' he said at last, 'that your Mr Makepeace may simply be fed up with the Big Brother attitude of Omega Oils and has decided to follow his own fancies without the benefit of their observation. It would be quite understandable – in character, it

39

appears. Is it important to find him, except for the sake of prestige? The new broom must find the last speck of dust?'

'Essential,' said Corkran dryly. 'Let me give you some basic data. A good geologist is like a good barman – anyone can serve and mix drinks but very few have genius. This one has the essential quality: he's a sort of human divining rod – a man who brings a sixth sense to bear on normal research into folds and strata and so on. The university-trained product is two a penny nowadays – the inexplicable creature with a built-in radar for oil or any other of the earth's riches is one in a million.'

He smiled at a wry thought before deciding to share it.

'I have all this from the best of my mentors in the firm – one of the most intelligent women I've ever met, and of course, very dislikeable. Brains and beauty are a rare combination and she certainly lacks the second quality. I educate myself respectfully if without pleasure. But the essential fact emerges. Omega think in millions, often in multiples of millions. Makepeace knows almost every secret of importance to the firm and if he opens his mouth to the wrong people it could have unthinkable consequences. The wrong people – which could mean the wrong nations – might negotiate themselves into far too strong a position for our liking.'

He began to cut a second cigar, giving the operation the attention it deserved.

'The world is pretty well mapped out where oil drilling concessions are concerned. Everyone knows who has the rights for potential operations but the matter is not as simple as that. A huge proportion of these concessions are valueless. It is more like exhibiting a thousand thimbles and knowing exactly which half-dozen conceal peas – a variation of the old racecourse game.'

'Could he be bribed? It sounds improbable but if you're talking in millions–'

Corkran shook his head. 'It is not a question of money in my view. I would describe him as a patriot who loathed civil servants, but never a traitor. The bribe, if it exists, could be the promise of adventure or of authority with an absolutely free hand. He still considers himself a young man, though he's within a month of my own age. Traces of the Boy Francis remain. There's a dozen or more years of work in him if he chooses. It really is very important to know what he is up to.'

He broke off, allowing the problem to linger in the air as if it were drifting in the smoke of the cigars.

'And you think I could help,' said Mr Campion at last. 'But why me? I would have thought you had a lot of experts at your disposal.'

Corkran was not graceful when asking favours. He put his thoughts in order and presented them as was his habit, in the form of a concise statement.

'The first point is one of pure snobbery: you can move around in circles where you would not be particularly remarked – you always specialized in behaving like a civilized nonentity. Makepeace, I fancy, would bury himself even deeper if he suspected his movements were known or his concealment penetrated, whatever he's up to. The second is that you are unlikely to succumb to a bribe and it is conceivable that one might be offered. And the third is that this is just the sort of problem you like.'

He eyed his friend quizzically from beneath twisted eyebrows. 'I haven't quite reached the end of the story, as far as it goes. There are some possible indications, if one knew how to read the augurs. Three reliable men have searched the Makepeace flat – he lives very comfortably and the rent is paid by banker's order, in what used to be called chambers, Hortin Mansions, in Albemarle Street. I have a list of what they thought of interest, though our friend was pretty careful about what he left behind. He had Big Brother well in mind. It could form a starting-point, however. The notes, by the way, are my own.'

He unfolded a sheet of paper from a note-case and pushed it across the coffee table.

Receipted Tailor's Bill; Manning and Collet, Dover Street, W1.

This is for a heavy tweed suit, missing from the flat. Pattern is available. N.B. Only a selection of the wardrobe has been removed. No tropical kit.

Boxes containing samples of earth from drilling, geological specimens, etc.

These are identified by the Company's code marks. They appear to come from areas in the Gulf of Aden, the Gulf of Mexico, the East African coast and Hong Kong where we had negative results. Similar specimens are recorded in the Company's office. No apparent reason for their retention, i.e. the presence of commercial minerals, precious stones, metals such as gold or copper. Any such discovery would come under the terms of his contract which are very tight, and it would be dishonest as well as nearly impossible to conceal it.

Roman coin, gold much eroded. Emperor Diocletian circa A.D. 300.

Found at back of drawer. Marine worm casing still adhering *(serpula Vernicularis)*. Not fully cleaned, suggesting a recent discovery, found under water.

Multibladed penknife. 'Smith, R. O.' scratched on side.

Fairly new. In box of oddments, screws, nails, light fittings, etc.

Bottle containing Lanolin.

Chemist's label says 'Ashburton MPS. Forest Hill SE.' Not a neighbourhood he would normally frequent.

Aqua-lung diving equipment of modern U.S. design, underwater cameras, etc.

All these items are very expensive which suggests ultimate intention to return. The large collection of under-water photographs does not appear to be of more than private interest.

Press-cutting.

On one side account of attack on a man called Morris Jay in the Hendon area by drunken youths from a dance hall. On the reverse Stock Exchange report including upward move of Omega shares. *Daily Globe* of March this year. Found under blotter.

Mr Campion considered the list for some time.

'Apart from the obvious deduction, my dear Watson, that our client was an Arabian beauty specialist who dabbled in marine biology, and gilt-edged stocks, there isn't a lot to go on,' he said at last. 'What do we know of Mr Morris Jay?'

Corkran was not amused.

'I had him checked, naturally. He runs an unexceptionable antique shop in Knightsbridge and buys for various other firms in the business. The attack seems to have been quite accidental, a piece of hooliganism, for he was not robbed although he had a fair sum of money on him – about seventy pounds. On the day before – a Friday – Omegas moved up a couple of points following a rumour that some drilling in our North Sea area had been outstandingly successful. The rumour was denied and the shares fell back on the Monday. There seems no reason for Makepeace to have been interested in either side of the cutting.'

'Yet he was. I should keep an eye on Mr Jay. Anything else? The Diocletian coin, for example?'

'It is valuable, but not remarkably rare. Makepeace could conceivably have found it among the stuff dredged up in the course of his official operations. He liked to work in the field, though he was too old for the job and there was really no necessity for it. Again, he was a keen diver and often spent his leave in the Mediterranean where several Roman wrecks have been found recently. There is a handsome amphora in his flat and one or two other treasures – a T'ang horse, for instance, and the foot from a marble statue, probably Greek. He wasn't a selective collector – the place is full of random curios picked up in various odd corners of the world where his work took him. Some of them are complete trash. The interest in the coin lies in the fact that it was left behind by accident – the rest of the drawer was empty and it was wedged into a crack at the back.'

'On the other hand,' said Mr Campion mildly, 'a Roman ship of the fourth century A.D. was discovered last year near the playing-fields of the Brett School in Suffolk at the mouth of the Brett river. "Smith R.O.'s penknife"? He could be Smith minor of the lower fourth.'

He closed his eyes.

'I know something about the Brett river – something I read yesterday. An odd item, now I come to think of it. A man's body was washed ashore there two days ago. He had been drowned but possibly banged on the head first. Max somebody – Max Newgate. The news value of the story rests in the fact that no one seems to know what he was doing down there. He was a hotel manager from somewhere in the Cotswolds.'

'Then you are interested?'

'Give me Smith minor's penknife and I'll see if I can return it to him.'

3

Coastguards

The sea, obeying mysterious dictates of wind and tide, erosion and retreat, had left the solitary cottage called 'Coastguards' nearly a mile inshore, so that it looked eastwards from what had once been the last outpost of land over the meandering Brett river and a placid wilderness of reed and fen. To the west the plateau, comfortably above sea level, is identifiable as playing-fields in winter by the tall 'H'-shaped goal posts of the Rugby game, in summer by sightscreens for cricket, and beyond them lie the range of buildings, white with steeply slated roofs, the Brett School. Its admirers claim it to be the most beautiful public school in England, for the architecture is Carolean with a strong local influence, giving it the mien of an idealized Flemish village.

Samuel Pepys, commemorated by a lead statue in the forecourt, is the true founder and benefactor, though the official credit goes to Charles II whose portrait by Antonio Verrio hangs in the dining-hall. It was the diarist rather than the king who understood that the problem of rebuilding the British Navy was as much a matter of men as of oak and shipyards: Brett was created at his instigation to supply a breed of midshipmen capable of becoming great seamen in the course of twenty years. Admirals Fortesque, Notley and Broadbent were all educated here and the school keeps its tradition, maintaining its own barge and paying more attention to the mastery of mathematics, which is the heart of navigation, than to what it regards as the lesser arts. Discipline is strict for this day and age, an autocratic survival which tends to prolong adolescence. Despite the nautical bias, groups of elms protect the playing-field and define the boundaries of the cricket pitch, being thicker on the southern side where the ground begins to slope towards the private quay. A group of small craft and the *Samuel Pepys* itself, the big Lowestoft barge, are regularly moored just off-shore.

A bell tent, a large wooden shed which might once have been a cricket pavilion, and two long mounds of newly turned earth made this area the focal point, for the distant buildings were blind-eyed, deserted as only a school can be in holidays, and in the long twilight a single lamp was beginning to assert itself at the mouth of the canvas cone.

Inside was a camp table on which were two office trays containing fragments of pottery and metal, string labels and an open logbook.

Despite the clutter the place was orderly, an advanced headquarters for operations.

Miss Anthea Peregrine, who was sitting behind the table in a green folding chair, had not moved for some time. Her chestnut curls were windblown but still trim and even in a dark blue shirt and faded jeans she remained unmistakably female.

Superstitious ancestors might have decided, not without reason, that she was engaged on an experiment in witchcraft. In the shallow pit outside the tent, where the skeleton imprint of what had once been a ship was shrouded beneath screens of canvas and tarpaulin, all work for the day was over and only a single figure remained squatting in the half light.

He will get up now, thought Miss Peregrine imperatively. He will get up now and come to me. He knows he has been breaking the rules and I want him to come to me deliberately, as if he had thought of it for himself. I want him to come here.

She bowed her head and began to write.

'Clench nails from port side strake and stem post...'

It was the season of moths. A yellow underwing began beating against the lamp and she looked up to find the expected figure standing in the opening, a tall young man shirtless and shaggy with a cricket sweater tied loosely round his neck. He was smiling and apologetic, uncertain of his reception and at nineteen still nearer a schoolboy than a man. In two years' time, said Miss Peregrine to herself, he'll be as handsome as Lucifer.

'I thought you called,' he said. 'But it might have been those damn gulls.'

One hand had been behind his back. He produced it now, holding a circle of decaying metal about the size of a fairground quoit.

'Any good?'

She put down her pen and surveyed him in a level stare which took the smile from his lips.

'You're a useless oaf. You know you're not supposed to touch that sort of thing if you suspect you're on to it. And you ought to have been away to your supper half an hour ago.'

His skin was too deeply sunburned to show if he was blushing.

'The Hag is out for the evening – gone off with Honker to the pics. It's cold scoff, all laid out and I can have it when I please. I thought you'd be interested in this ringlet. Part of the rigging? I marked where I found it.'

'I should hope so. Put it down.' She sighed as if exasperated by the stupidity of her visitor.

'You should try being your age. You're going to Cambridge in a couple of months and your slang still belongs to the lower school. Miss Lewthwaite is not to be referred to as the Hag, by you or by any other senior, even out of term.'

'Sorry. My landlady, the senior matron of this empty mausoleum, has left me a cold collation. She is being escorted to the animated kinematograph in Orwell by Mr Deakin, the head purser, and I am a free man at least until midnight. I'm just a lodger now, not a scholar, you know. Is there anything I can do for you?'

Miss Peregrine considered the proposition from a position of strength.

She was not prepared to admit the young man to the freemasonry of the age-group to which they both belonged. He would have to wait for that privilege, until she decided to allow him to grow up and open his eyes. In the meantime she was deeply contented with the situation, certain of herself and unwilling to share her intentions.

'Yes,' she said at last. 'Yes, there is. You went down to the village this morning. Is there any news about that man they found in the river?'

'I thought you knew all about him. The police spent hours with you. They say you stayed in his hotel where Matty died, so presumably he was coming to see you. Was he?'

'He wasn't – or at least he never arrived. A nasty little creep. If he was interested in

51

anyone here it must have been Mr Matthews. But as he certainly knew he was dead, it must have been the background he was spying out. Didn't anyone notice him in the village? The poor little runt was so head-waitery and neat that he would be bound to attract attention.'

'Not a soul, so far as I heard. I spent an hour in the Mainsail, which is very dull now it isn't out of bounds, and didn't really gather a thing. They say you're going to be his heiress and he was a secret millionaire, if there is such a bird. Any truth in it?'

She shook her head in a show of anger which he found chilling.

'You're an impertinent ass. You shouldn't listen to idiot gossip.'

'Sorry,' he said. 'You asked me, so I told you. Oh, there was one other thing, but if you're not interested ... it's only gossip, after all.'

'Well?'

'They don't seem to know how he got here. If he came by train to Orwell – a horrible roundabout way from a place like Great Burdon – he would have hired a taxi or taken the bus. Then someone would have noticed him, because between Orwell and Brett everyone knows everyone, but nobody did as far as I can gather. So he must have come by car. Yet apparently there is no car lying about. They're searching all over the

52

place for one. I have this, by the way, from Mrs Fellows of the Mainsail who is in close touch with Mrs Catt, who is a sister of Mrs Martlesham the wife of P.C. Martlesham who is believed – inaccurately, I imagine – to be in charge of the investigation. There's glory for you.'

She pondered the information and, as if she felt herself softening towards the young man, reasserted her authority.

'Put your sweater on. It's getting cold. And you'd better push off now to your supper. I've quite a bit of marking up to do, so don't hang about.'

He made to obey her but still lingered in front of the table, running his fingers through untidy brown hair.

'You're bothered – worried – aren't you? It is because of old Matty?'

'Of course. This hotel man, Newgate, must have come here to try to find out something about Mr Matthews. Someone didn't want to have him nosing around so they pushed him in the river. The police know that well enough: they're quite on the ball. So who wouldn't be worried?'

'Do you think he went up to Coastguards? Old Matty's furniture and belongings are up there, aren't they?'

'Your guess is as good as mine. His stuff is all dumped there – some more came today – but there's nothing to suggest that it's been messed about. It's all in packing-cases anyhow.'

'Now he's dead who does it belong to?'

She shrugged her shoulders.

'Nobody knows. I'm trying to find out and so are the lawyers. Meantime the rent is paid, the place is really nothing to do with me any longer, except that I have the keys. I'm just waiting to see who is really authorized to take over. You can tell that to Mrs Fellows, Mrs Catt and Mrs Martlesham next time you're at the Mainsail.'

'I will. I liked the old warhorse. A pity to drop off the hook like that when he was all set for a bit of fun. He knew a thing or two about digging too – the theoretical side of it, anyway. I never realized how a river could change course overnight, though I suppose it's obvious. He was rather good at explaining things. Do you think he was rich – rolling in it, I mean – like they say?'

'I've no idea,' said Miss Peregrine sharply. 'None of my business, nor yours, come to that. You get back to your house now if you're going to do an early shift.'

'There's no hurry. I'm going in to Orwell on my bike in the morning to collect young Woodhouse who's joining the dig. Commander King is S.N.O.B. [Senior Naval Officer on board] for the day. I suppose I couldn't wait for you?'

'You'd just be a nuisance. I'll see you tomorrow, two fifteen sharp.'

He was nettled and wheeled sharply away. 'Good night, then.'

Had he looked back instead of plunging into the twilight he would have seen that the girl had moved to the mouth of the tent to watch him go. She had switched off the lamp so that without the glare she could catch the last of his back as he strode towards the school, his hands deep in his pockets and his feet kicking angrily at anything in his path.

When he was out of sight she turned back into the tent, her arm outstretched to find the makeshift switch which hung from the centre pole, and paused immobile. Gulls disturbed by the departing figure were still wheeling and mewing but the new sound did not belong to the evening. She waited, listening, her head on one side. Somewhere in the direction of Coastguards a dog barked.

The light was fading now and the cottage, a low bungalow beside what looked like a small Martello tower but was in fact the base of an old lighthouse, was no more than a white blur on the horizon.

She closed the tent, tying the flaps securely for the night and listened again but the sound was not repeated. If a dog barks once, she thought, and is silent again, then he is not alone. His demands, whatever they are, have been met. She picked up her satchel, felt for a pocket torch and set off by the footpath.

Previous owners had made varying and partially successful efforts to protect the cottage from the coastal wind. On the northern side a screen of poplars marked the boundary and a yew hedge, dark and unkempt, lined the approach from landward. It was a remote and private place, giving up its secrets only when a visitor was within a few yards of the shuttered windows. Miss Peregrine approached by way of a gap in the defences where a topiarist had made a half-hearted assault on the yew. A removal van, which earlier in the day had delivered packing-cases, sat parked very neatly between the wall of the cottage and the stunted tower so that in the half light it could have been part of the building. She had supervised the unloading operation and was surprised to find that it was still there.

The keys were kept hidden in the casing of the yard pump and she fumbled for them now, her other hand gripping the unlighted torch.

Presently she unlocked the back door and stepped inside. The dog, if it was still there, remained silent.

4

Missing Link

'Mr Albert Campion?' said Superintendent Appleyard of the Suffolk C.I.D. 'Pleased to meet you.'

He was not speaking the truth and made no attempt to conceal the fact. His visitor had presented himself at an office in the Orwell police station at an inopportune moment but a forcefully-worded introduction had made the interview impossible to evade.

'Charlie Luke of the Yard seems to be an old friend of yours. I like to oblige a colleague even if I only see him once in five years.' He paused and added as a minimum gesture of politeness. 'How is he these days?'

'All zeal,' said Mr Campion mildly. 'He sent you his regards.'

'Very civil of him.'

The superintendent was a large man, close-cropped and deliberately unobtrusive in his grey suit and grey striped tie. Only the eyebrows, black as ebony, made the face memorable. A touch of amiability would have suggested a bank manager or a successful insurance agent but the quality was missing, leaving him impassive, a man accustomed to waiting for information on which he could build.

The courtesies were at an end.

'I came,' said the visitor, 'about this man who was found in the river, Max Newgate. I have certain interest in his movements. Charles Luke said that it was your case and he felt sure you would receive me.'

The superintendent sniffed.

'The position, as I see it, sir,' he said, 'is not what I can tell you but what you can tell me. Did you know the deceased, for example?'

'I see a connection between him and this district.'

'And so do I. That's my job, Mr Campion, and I'm none too clear what yours is, if I may say so. What can you tell me about this Mr Newgate which I don't already know? I'd be glad to learn. We've spoken to his staff at the Drover's Arms in Great Burdon and to Miss Peregrine, a local lady who stayed there about a week ago. How do you think you can help?'

The ice remained unbroken. A fresh approach was clearly necessary if any progress was to be achieved. Mr Campion took off his spectacles and spoke with more force than his appearance suggested.

'If your Mr Newgate was just a nosey parker who came down here out of curiosity about his hotel clients and happened to fall into the river because his foot slipped, then we're both wasting our time. If he was banged on the head first, which is murder by any reckoning, then there's a small but untidy packet of trouble on the horizon.'

'Who says so?'

'I do.'

The superintendent, as was his habit, was weighing up the situation, balancing his dislike of the visitor and the senior London policeman who had introduced him against the chances of antagonizing a witness who might be useful.

'You don't answer my question. I said: "How do you think you can help the investigation?" Whether it's accidental death or something else is my business just at the moment and I'm a busy man.'

As if to emphasize the point the telephone on his desk began to buzz like an important beetle. He lifted the receiver.

'Appleyard. Yes... About ten minutes ago. He's certain of that, is he? Wait...'

He glanced at Campion.

'Your car is parked outside? A grey Jaguar? And you came alone?'

As his visitor nodded he scribbled a note, tore it from the pad and returned to the instrument. 'Yes, if Coleman isn't making a fool of himself. No ... well, there's no law against it, that I know of. But tell the mobile

59

boys to keep their eyes open if he moves off. I'll be free in a couple of minutes.'

He rang off but continued to stare at the instrument as if it had something to add. Finally he picked up the slip of paper and tossed it to Campion, across his desk. He made up his mind, clearly against his first intentions, and proceeded with caution if not grace.

'You may need that later on. At the moment I'm going to make a confession to you. It'll be common knowledge in an hour or two but it might help you to see things my way. As from now we're treating this as a case of murder. Is that what you wanted to know?'

'You've some new evidence?'

'We found what we were looking for, if that's what you mean. Newgate drove down here in a car which belonged to a man called Matthews. It had been left in the garage of his hotel when the guest – who was coming to live hereabouts – died. Newgate was simply delivering it, you might have thought, though he seems to have gone a funny way about it. It was found off Brett Ness at low tide this morning. There's a bit of a cliff there and it had been pushed over the edge. It's barely a mile from the cottage which Matthews had rented and the sand below is on the treacherous side – quick mud, in fact. It makes a likely dumping ground for all sorts of rubbish. Dozens of crocks are buried there but they don't get there by chance. They have to be pushed or driven up the last few yards and toppled over. Newgate wouldn't have come halfway across England just for that. Besides it was a good car, a Rover, and worth quite a bit. No, sir. It was done to cover up the fact that he'd been here and it was done after he was dead. It all adds up. Whoever killed him – and we now know that there was a someone – removed all the identification he could find from the body, labels, pocket-book and so on, everything in fact except his shoes. They happen to have been hand-made and we got the name through the maker's last number.'

He sat back and pulled his chin into his collar.

'Now, Mr Campion, I'm a busy man as you can see. Can you help me at all, or are you and Mr Luke wasting my time?'

The visitor sighed. He had replaced his glasses and was staring absently into the distance.

'Dear me. As you say, very conclusive. It makes the late Mr Matthews a most interesting figure. He's the key to your problem, Superintendent, and if you want my advice you'll concentrate on that angle. Did you discover much about him?'

'Enough to satisfy me. Matthews was Matthews and nobody else, if that's what you're getting at. You can't have mystery men roaming round the country under assumed names these days – not for long anyhow. The income tax inspector won't have it, even if the bank manager will. He was a retired engineer in building – factory construction – they think. He worked for a Belgian firm in East Africa and got a regular pension paid into his account at Burdon. Comfortable, you know, but not rolling in it according to the local tax man who dealt with him. It was no secret that he was looking for somewhere to settle and in the meantime the Drover's Arms was as near as he got to a permanent base. He's been around for about four years off and on. Subscribed to the cricket club, the hospital, the church rebuilding fund and the like.

'The doctor was by no way of being a friend and he had warned him about his heart. We've had a word with the Coroner's officer, my men have talked with the hotel people and I've interviewed Miss Peregrine. Not a helpful young lady but then she takes after her father who's a schoolmaster. He's in France just now with a party of boys. He's the odd man out in that outfit, not being a naval type, and the girl is what they call cool these days. In my language that means she's a self-possessed bossy little madam who treats everyone as if they were kids in her father's house.'

He drew breath and regarded his visitor

with an inquiring eye which managed to indicate that the concessions were at an end.

'Do you think you can add to that?'

'Probably not. Except for the lady we seem to have covered the same ground. And so have a lot of other people.'

'And who might they be?'

Mr Campion's smile was diffident. 'People like myself who are interested in discovering the background of the late Mr Matthews. Newgate, poor chap, seems to have had the same sort of inquiring mind, though I don't see where he fits into the picture.' He hesitated. 'You're interested in facts, not theories?'

'Get on with it, sir. I haven't a lot of time.'

'My bet would be that Newgate was killed at Coastguards or thereabouts by someone who was on the same errand, but acting independently. His body must have been dumped before they found the car. They could identify it by the key if they searched the body. No doubt you have reached the same conclusion.'

'I have. And what was so special about Mr Matthews to your way of thinking?'

Campion stood up.

'A very good question,' he said. 'I can lay my hand on my heart and say that I don't know the answer. I'm making some inquiries about a man who's gone missing and it occurred to me that he might have been calling himself Matthews. You appear to have put paid to that thought. By the way, this chit you gave me suggests the number of a car.'

'SVX 368 D, a green Cortina, driven by a man called Scott – Ginger Scott – about whom we happen to know a thing or two. He was recognized by one of my men who had some dealings with him. It looks as if he's been following you and is hanging about outside just round the corner. Did you know that?'

'In fact, I did,' Mr Campion was apologetic. 'He's been shadowing me ever since I left Great Burdon early this morning. A very indifferent performance. I was hoping for a chat with him later on.'

'It'll have to wait, sir. You've given me an idea. I'll do my own chatting first, if you don't mind.' He picked up the telephone and nodded to his visitor without extending his hand.

'Good-bye, Mr Campion. Very much obliged, I'm sure. Give my compliments to Mr Luke.'

5

The Trespasser

When Miss Peregrine entered Coastguards she closed the door quietly behind her and waited in the narrow passage which bisected the cottage. The front and back doors faced each other at opposite ends and the entrance to the living-room was in the centre to her left.

To her right was the kitchen, a low-ceilinged primitive place with a brick floor and a stone sink, shuttered and dark despite the whitewashed walls. The three packing-cases which had been delivered during the morning stood beside the scrubbed table and she explored each of them with her torch. They had not been disturbed.

Outside the second door she paused again but the silence was unbroken. She lifted the latch and stepped inside.

Immediately she was aware that the room was not empty. The warmth and scent of humanity in a confined space came to her as clearly as a warning whisper in the ear.

She stood very still, gripping the unlit torch, listening. A dog growled and was abruptly silenced. She heard his paws scrape the floorboards as his head was jerked. She counted the invisible intruders, sensing their presence in the darkness. Two men were behind her and a third was drawing slow asthmatic breath somewhere in the gloom with the dog.

'Mr Porteous,' said Miss Peregrine at last. 'If you don't turn the light on I shall shine my torch straight in your face.'

There was no immediate reply but a rustle betrayed a movement near her elbow.

'She's alone. O.K. to switch on?' The voice, soft and unemotional, was answered from the far corner.

'You may do that. Miss Peregrine, please stand quite still until my dog accepts you as a visitor. You two may leave us briefly, but perhaps one of you – William, I suggest William – will remain within reasonable distance.'

A single unshaded bulb which dangled from a hook in the ceiling was not kind to the room or its contents. It emphasized the blue shadows on the jowls of the man sitting in a high winged chair and gave the jumble of furniture and packing-chests the dispirited air of a junk shop which has gone out of business. An Alsatian dog on a leash stood by the ponderous figure, his hackles alert. Behind the girl a latch clicked and in the brick passage retreating footsteps dwindled.

'Why are you trespassing?' Miss Peregrine

demanded angrily.

The tinted glasses gave no indication that the fat man was returning her stare. He moved one hand from his stick to brush dust from his thigh and wheezed as if the effort was exhausting.

'You are a problem to me, Miss Peregrine – a problem and a great nuisance. Certainly I am intruding and without authority. I make no apology and it is difficult to see what you can do by way of redress, of retort. But since you are here I will make my position clear. I will go further – I will make you an offer which I strongly advise you to accept.'

The girl did not answer him directly. She turned her head to look round the room, apparently making an inventory. When the inspection was complete she eased the satchel from her shoulder, and balanced herself on the edge of a table, one foot on a large cabin trunk.

'You're the second or third nosy parker to come snooping around here – or perhaps you've been here before? What are you trying to steal?'

'I said I would make you an offer. Shall I disclose it?' She shook her head.

'Just get out.'

'You are suspicious. That is understandable, it is entirely natural in the light of my intrusion. But your opinion of me is unimportant, irrelevant. We must – both of us

– disregard it.

'Do you know you are an heiress, Miss Peregrine? I think you do. I think you had a letter this morning from a solicitor in Burdon saying that Mr Matthews had made you his sole legatee. If I may make a guess, an informed guess, I should say, you inherit a sum of about five thousand pounds and such papers and personal effects as can be found. Do you confirm that?'

She stood up as if she were preparing to go and at the sudden move the dog growled an unmistakable threat. Porteous caressed him into silence.

'You are likely to be here for some time, until I have justified my own visit, in fact. You are not in a position to hurry away and raise an alarm. That is out of the question, not to be envisaged. The letter I spoke of is probably in your handbag at the moment. I shall make that assumption and I shall base what I propose to say on its contents.'

Miss Peregrine lifted the sling of the satchel on to her shoulder.

'You,' she said and paused to choose her words, 'are a cracking bore. You remind me of something out of a very old film. The smelly types who were standing behind me ought to be one-eyed mulattoes whose tongues have been cut out. You should be your age – God knows you look old enough.'

The sting seemed to please the man in the

chair. He cleared his throat with a rasping wheeze that was almost a chuckle.

'Have you ever been compared to a cat, Miss Peregrine?' he said when the process was complete. 'You remind me strongly – inescapably – of one. Cats have a certain complacency, an appearance of arrogance which invites retaliation, possibly cruelty. One feels an urge to impinge on their lives, to enforce a respect which is never forthcoming. They flirt with violence and either sneer or spit when it occurs. I must restrain the instinct, the considerable temptation, to discover your reactions under stress.

'I said I would make you an offer, so apply your mind and try to free it from obstinacy, from prejudice. Think of the total value of Mr Matthews's possessions here and anything else which you may inherit, excepting only the existing funds and cash which are of no interest to me. I mean every other item, every book, trinket or scrap of paper which comes to you. Assume if you like that the furniture is all genuine antique and that the silver is Georgian of the best period. Make a good price, regardless of facts. Then double it. I will meet your demands without quibble or question however grotesque they may sound. Do I have your attention, your interest?'

The girl had not moved whilst Porteous was speaking. Now she perched herself again on the table, her head on one side examining the intruder contemptuously. Her voice was cold and deliberate.

'You're not getting the message, are you? As far as I'm concerned you can go to hell. I don't want to speak to you or to listen to anything you say. If I were you I'd get out whilst the going's good. The police are trying to find out who killed a man near here and I shall tell them all about you just as soon as I can. Short of killing me – which would be damn silly and get you nowhere – you can't stop me. Why don't you get lost?'

Porteous drew a breath which expanded his considerable form like a bull-frog and expelled it in a long sigh.

'Very like a cat. You tempt me, you invite sadism, but I must control my urge towards that pleasure. Very well then, you will not bargain and I doubt if you would change your mind under pressure. A great mistake, Miss Peregrine, because your benefactor Matthews has attracted a lot of attention from others besides myself. One of them at least is not above violence, as you apparently realize. Have you ever considered how vulnerable, how completely unprotected, you are?'

He unclasped a small plump hand from his stick and raised a finger.

'I shall assume a negative answer. Let me put an idea, a suggestion or two in your head. Your father is a short-sighted man with a certain vanity about using glasses. He prefers

70

contact lenses in front of his students. Yet he goes climbing with them, explores potholes, and swims like a man half his age. He could meet with an accident which would be simple to arrange. Again, you have a young friend, an understandable admirer. He drives incautiously and the brakes of his motor-cycle might fail at any moment, given a little assistance. You yourself could be attacked, savaged by an ill-tempered dog like mine – and you would find yourself marked, scarred for life. The possibilities are innumerable – stimulating to the imagination – and I have only cited a few elementary examples.'

She returned his stare without emotion.

'You really are an extraordinarily stupid man. If I won't be bribed into doing what I don't intend to do why should I give in to threats? Why are you interested in Mr Matthews anyway? You said you'd never met him. What are you after?'

'Information about a business matter. I shall not put it more lucidly since the pos-session of such knowledge could be very dangerous to you despite your assumption of indifference.'

He leaned forward. 'I am not exaggerating, young lady. If you do not believe me, con-sider what happened to the man who came prowling here, thinking to act on his own. My offer will bring you complete safety and a large sum of money. It would be most unwise not to accept.'

'You can puff till you burst,' said Miss Peregrine flatly, 'for all I care. I want to go now. Are you going to try to stop me?'

Porteous sat back in the chair which was creaking under his weight. He rubbed the inner corners of his eyes between chubby fingers and relaxed.

'I have given some thought to that. I wish you no particular harm at the moment – you are courting enough trouble without any action I may have to take later on. No, you cannot be trusted alone tonight. I could not rely on you to keep silent even if you could be persuaded to give your word. A promise made under duress is quite valueless. I am living a nomadic life at the moment and I have a caravan of sorts outside this cottage – the type of headquarters a general might use in time of war. You saw it this morning, an unremarkable furniture van at a superficial glance. It is really extremely comfortable and excellently equipped.

'You will be dispatched to some conveniently remote spot and I advise you to get some sleep on the way. In the morning you will find your car waiting for you and you may drive home just as soon as you are able to locate a petrol station, for the tank will have been emptied.

'I don't know what explanation you will give for your absence overnight but if you reappear, as you will, in your own car, then perhaps your young friend can be persuaded to take the blame? It is open to you, of course, to go to the authorities with your version of our meeting tonight but my pantechnicon is designed like a chameleon – it changes its colours and its identification without difficulty. You may elect to describe me to the police but even if they believe your very unlikely story before they can take action they will have to locate me. I am not a resident of this country – my health does not permit more than an occasional visit – and I am by nature, by the nature of my business, secretive, elusive. Should I need to meet you again, you will be informed, but without preliminary warning.'

He leaned back in the chair, straightening his spine against the cushions.

'Now, you have a choice. My aides can truss you up like a parcel and with the help of a gentle narcotic you will be made to mind your manners. That way will involve a certain amount of inconvenience, of discomfort. Alternatively, I can offer coffee, sandwiches, a well-sprung couch and modern sanitation. You could of course take a petty revenge by being destructive in my cabin but if you do I shall allow one of my friends, who is in the habit of handling – of controlling – a potentially dangerous dog, to discipline you. He would enjoy the opportunity but it would be most unsuitable to your dignity. What is your decision?'

Miss Peregrine took her time before answering. She stood up and wandered round the room, ignoring the figure in the chair, giving her attention to the packing-cases and the disorganized collection of furniture.

'You won't find whatever it is you're looking for, you know,' she said at last. 'I don't think you've got the brains. You're too bogus altogether. But I don't want to be tied up and left on the railway line before the express thunders by, so I'll eat your sandwiches. I hope your coffee isn't drugged with some secret poison unknown to science.'

Porteous released his asthmatic chuckle, recovering his breath in a series of slow intakes which gradually restored his normal wheeze.

'Very sensible, very practical. A modern pragmatic approach to a problem which has no other civilized solution. I expected, I anticipated nothing else. Now you will trot along with my Mr William – with whom I suggest, I advise, that you should not attempt to be witty, to my caravan. It has a most ingeniously concealed entrance through the back of the pantechnicon which appears to be full of goods in transit. You will appreciate the deception, you may even enjoy it. But before you go I will attempt to put an idea in your mind, a point which may not have impinged upon your considerable intelligence. Can you deduce it?'

'I don't intend to try.'

'Then I will spell it out for you. You disappoint me, but perhaps I am expecting too much, perhaps I am confusing pertness with perception. This is the crux of the matter. In an enterprise such as I am engaged upon, which concerns major interests, sums quite beyond your imagination, you are expendable – as unimportant as an incautious mouse who thinks it can circumnavigate a tray and get to the cheese unharmed. Good night, Miss Peregrine.'

He tapped his stick sharply on the floor and the latch clicked behind her. The dog barked a salute and was silenced. Two men had come into the room and she turned to look them over unwaveringly, searching for an identification which she could memorize. They were large unremarkable workmen in boiler suits but the elder, powerful and red-faced, had a small white scar on his upper lip and the younger was balding with round steel spectacles of great magnification giving him the appearance of a sufferer from goitre. Porteous addressed himself to the senior man.

'William, you will take this young lady to my cabin, where she has undertaken to behave herself, but as a precaution, an act of prudence, you will blindfold her on the way. Not your handkerchief, which might prove offensive to her, but the scarf out of her bag. She may attempt to elude you once outside but the process will be difficult if she is sightless.

'She may have my sandwiches and you will make her some coffee. Lock her in and tether the dog just outside the door. He will no doubt alert us if she decides to act indiscreetly. As a further precaution you will also lock up the communication system. If she causes any damage or tries to make a nuisance of herself you have my permission, my authority, to deal with her as you would with any other recalcitrant child. Put her over your knee and destroy her comfort and her dignity.'

Miss Peregrine allowed herself to be led away without resistance. When she released the scarf over her eyes she was standing in a cubicle containing a large bunk, a fitted desk and a chair designed to suit the proportions of its owner, a comfortable cabin where everything of interest was concealed behind locked panels.

There were smoked salmon sandwiches, trim and inviting on a tray, and she was grateful when the man addressed as William appeared an hour after they had been consumed bearing a vacuum flask containing coffee.

She was asleep before the first cup was empty.

A dawn wind blowing fitfully down the back of her neck roused her to chilly discomfort and she stirred uneasily, aware that if she attempted to move too quickly her head might swim. Cautiously she flexed her toes, rubbed her eyes and ran a hand through her hair. Her mouth was unpleasantly dry. Life returned to her limbs, bringing pins and needles in its wake.

She was sitting, she realized, in her own car with a rug tucked around her and, through the mist, trees were beginning to emerge dripping damply with early dew. The little Renault was parked on the grass verge of a narrow road between dense woodland and the petrol-tank was undoubtedly empty. At the third attempt to start the engine she gave up, remembering ruefully what Porteous had prophesied. There was nothing for it but to walk until she found assistance.

She climbed out stiffly and looked about her. The road was well metalled but gave no indication where it might lead. Civilization could not be far off, for the remains of a picnic were scattered under the nearest oak.

The hoot of a motor horn repeated several times made her turn sharply. Behind her a second car sat solid and reassuring twenty yards down the lane, its outline only just discernible in the haze.

She began to walk unsteadily towards it,

stamping her feet to bring back circulation. As she drew level a window was lowered and a tousled grey head thrust out. 'Ha! So there you are.'

'Oh, it's you,' she said. 'I've a terrible head this morning. But don't worry – you're not really a surprise. I'm not going to faint or burst into tears. I was half expecting you.'

6

Encounter

The excavation of the Roman ship had attracted the interest of several groups of holiday-makers. They stood around the long pit, bright as scraps from a dressmaker's work box in the afternoon sun, watching the dedicated toilers as they lifted the earth delicately to uncover the past. A party of young men who had arrived by water called to friends in the hollow, and at the mouth of the bell tent, where the camp table had been set, three experts were discussing an object closely resembling a rusty horseshoe.

Mr Campion left his car amongst half-a-dozen others near the site and watched the proceedings for some time before he wandered off down the track leading to Coastguards. The approach to the cottage was by way of a pockmarked road which skirted the school grounds on the far side and as he drew closer a police car disappeared into the drive behind the yew hedge, preceded by a motor-cyclist in uniform.

To the right of the track the ground sloped gently upwards covered by a scrub of blackberry bushes and saplings bent by the coastal wind. It made an uncomfortable but satisfactory hideout. Mr Campion applied himself to the business of observation with the aid of a small pair of binoculars.

Two cars and a police van were parked outside the open door of the cottage and in the overgrown garden a systematic search of the ground by several uniformed figures was in progress.

Shutters had been latched back outside the windows and through the lenses it was possible to see that the inside of the panes was being dusted for fingerprints. An occasional flash of light showed that a photographer was at work. Superintendent Appleyard, who appeared briefly at the door to call one of his men, was evidently directing operations.

After some minutes he emerged again from the opening, followed by two men carrying a large packing-case which was loaded into the van. A driver approached him and he took a radio telephone call, leaning against the door of his car and cradling the instrument between cheek and shoulder as he lit a cigarette.

A sudden crash of undergrowth, very close to the watcher, made him spin round. Behind him stood a young man who had evidently taken a considerable jump to reach his present unsteady foothold. He regained his balance and glowered, his face bright with anger, his fists clenched.

Mr Campion contemplated six feet of tensed muscle and suspicion from behind his oversize spectacles.

'I hope,' he said mildly, 'that I do not disturb you.'

'Who are you? Why are you snooping around?'

'Curiosity. A common complaint – we both seem to suffer from it.'

The newcomer was not softened. He measured the older man's height, still prepared to attack, decided that they were imperfectly matched by reason of age, but persisted with his interrogation.

'You've no business here. What do you want?'

Mr Campion proffered his binoculars.

'If you want a closer look, borrow these. Something rather odd seems to be going on at Coastguards. Do you know what they're up to?'

The offer was too tempting to be ignored. The boy took the glasses, adjusted them professionally and made a long survey of the activity around the cottage.

'Police,' he said at last. 'I wondered how long they'd be before they caught on. It was bloody obvious that they'd have to search the place.' A smile crept into the corners of his eyes and he held out the binoculars. 'Thanks – a damn good pair considering their size.'

81

'You know about the trouble?'

'A chap was killed there. That's what I think.' Suspicion returned to his eyes. 'Who are you, anyway? A journalist or something?'

'I think you could call me a spy,' said Mr Campion modestly, 'but on your side of the fence. I suppose you didn't know Mr Matthews by any chance?'

'I knew him all right. I liked him a lot. He was going to help with the ship, you know. Rotten luck, dying like that.'

'The worst. Was Miss Peregrine very upset?'

The inquiry evidently touched a sore spot for the young man looked away, shrugging his shoulders. His voice, casual by intention, sounded petulant.

'I've no idea. She doesn't confide in me – or anyone else, come to that.'

'Some women,' said Mr Campion, speaking as one adult male to another, 'are like that. They feel that secrets add to their importance. Is she a friend of yours?'

'Sort of. She's the daughter of old Foggy Peregrine who was my housemaster at Brett. I've left, you know – I'm just playing out time before I go up to Cambridge. My people live in New Zealand.'

Mr Campion took a long shot.

'You don't happen to be Smith, R.O.?'

Surprise chased the air of sophistication from the boy's face.

'That's me. But I don't know you. Is it any of your business?'

'In a way,' said Mr Campion, 'it is. Among other things, I came here to return your penknife.'

Superintendent Appleyard had been called a great many abusive names in his time, the scale ranging from the 'cold-blooded bastard' of his enemies via 'obstinate pig-head' from his colleagues to 'graceless lout', the opinion of his Chief Constable. No one had ever suggested the word inefficient, for each category was honest according to its own peculiar standards.

He stood in the centre of the room which took up most of the ground floor of the cottage called Coastguards, his thumbs hooked into his trouser belt and his head on one side, contemplating a scene of chaos which would have dismayed a lesser man and driven most women to hysteria. The fact that there was a suggestion of order in the destruction added menace to the atmosphere. It was as if a vicious child had systematically broken up the contents of a doll's house, piece by piece, stacking the discarded wreckage in order to keep an area clear for the process, so that nothing escaped. In one corner stood a range of picture-frames, their backs separated but the glass intact. Against the wall under a long window looking out to sea, chairs were ranged each with the seat ripped open and the stuffing scattered. A tallboy gaped like a toothless skull whilst the drawers were piled neatly enough beside it. A dozen packing-cases had been opened and their contents, silver, crockery and ornaments, occupied a half of the floor space whilst the wood shavings and old newspapers which had been used as packing were massed in a heap in another corner. Candlesticks, twisted and broken, lay in a pile with broken ornaments but cups and plates remained intact. Two experts, armed with a remarkably archaic camera, were taking photographs.

'Systematic,' said Superintendent Appleyard. 'I wonder if they found what they were looking for? Probably they did. Three cases haven't been touched.'

His senior supporter, Sergeant Foss, a prim clerical figure who based his wardrobe on the style favoured by his superior officer, scratched the back of his neck, his head on one side.

'Not straight robbery, anyhow. Some of this silver is quite valuable, or was before it was ruined. Those candlesticks...'

Appleyard swung on one heel and kicked at a bundle of straw by his feet.

'Paper – letters – documents. That's the target area.' He returned to Foss. 'You know how my mind's working. Why else would Newgate have come here?'

'Blackmail?'

'That's about the size of it. Newgate must have unearthed some dirt about this chap Matthews whilst he was at the Drover – it would be easy enough in his job and he's probably done it before. He had a name for being a nosy parker. We'll check on that angle. As I see it he wanted just that little bit extra – some additional hold – a solid proof of some sort – document. He came down here to find it and that was the end of the chapter. Go on from there.'

'But Matthews was dead, so he couldn't have been the sucker. The girl Peregrine, perhaps?'

Appleyard clicked his tongue.

'Little Miss Knowall. She's not around today, but she's got a lot of explaining to do at my next session with her. She knows more than she lets on, she's so poker-faced I get that feeling. But it wouldn't be her own secret whatever it was – not at her age and with her background. She fits in somewhere, so we'll have to get that bit of the jigsaw out of her.'

'There were three men on this job last night. Three men and a dog. They've found the dog's prints and its droppings. A big chap according to Arthur here who's by way of being an expert. And what about those three sealed cases? You think they stopped the search before they got to them?'

'Maybe,' said Appleyard blankly. 'Could be. One possibility, like I said. The other is that they brought them with the van – it was seen here yesterday afternoon – and that was their excuse for calling. The contents – they came from the Burdon hotel, by the labels – could have been searched on the way. I'm checking on that but it won't lead anywhere. You can see what happened.' He became more animated, using his hands to emphasize the picture. 'She was here, you know, to let them in. "Where do you want this lot put, miss? Very good miss. To me Charlie, from you. Thank you, miss. You don't mind if we take our tea-break here, miss? We've a long way to go yet." I'd say they hung around until evening and then made a good job of the search when they weren't likely to be interrupted.'

Foss was gloomy.

'It doesn't help us much. It's a long stretch to see the girl hitting Newgate over the head because she caught him here, thinking he was dead and then dropping him into the tideway – no, that's a non-starter. A two-man job at the least. Now we know there were three of them here yesterday – one of them using a walking-stick – and a dog. It's clear as mud to me, right now. It brings us back to Matthews.'

He paused, unwilling to court one of those snubs for which Appleyard was notorious, but decided to risk it. 'That chap, Ginger

Scott. You had him in this morning for suspected loitering. Has he any connection?'

The Superintendent shook his head. 'Right off the beam. A red herring you could call him and that's not a bad description either. He was tailing this pal of Charlie Luke's who turned up this morning, hoping to pick my brains. An industrial espionage inquiry as I read it. Campion – that was the fellow's name – is looking for some V.I.P. in commerce who's vanished, no doubt for good reasons of his own. Campion must be a long way from home because he thought his missing man might be Matthews. That cock won't fight. I sent him packing and I don't thank Charlie Luke Esquire for wasting my time. What we want is another fact or two – a new lead.'

Sergeant Foss picked up the head of a melancholy Staffordshire pottery dog from a pile of broken china, shook it, and put it down again.

'This Roman ship,' he said. 'Matthews was mad keen on it, they say. Digging up wine jugs, old iron and so on. Could there be something in that – treasure, gold ornaments like the one at Sutton Hoo?'

Appleyard considered the suggestion with a gravity which relieved his subordinate.

'No,' he said at last. 'No. There's never less than six people on the job when they're digging, with someone superior in charge – generally a schoolmaster or some other egghead – and as often as not an official from the Orwell Museum lurking around. Whenever they find anything there's a song and a dance, even if it's only a Roman toothpick. What I'm looking for, Fred, is a nice dirty little twentieth-century scandal, a family secret or the like – something that rich relations would pay to keep quiet. Though in this day and age I can't get around to imagining anything anyone would pay fourpence for. But it must be there, if we go deep enough. We...'

He broke off. A uniformed policeman had put his head round the door leading to the yard.

'A call from Orwell for you, sir. Will you take it?'

In the absence of his chief Foss turned to the photographer and his assistant who were dusting the panel of an inner door for prints. He watched unhappily for some time, reflecting that they at least understood their share of the business. He envied them.

'Getting anything?'

'You could say damn all. The place has been cleaned up very carefully. If we do all the crockery and silver down here it'll take a week. We're sending the likely items to our own lab. A funny mixture if you ask me – foreign junk mostly but one or two bits of good stuff. By the look of it some has never been opened since the day it was packed in

Mexico or Singapore or wherever. Wrapped in newspapers from all over the world, ten or twenty years out of date. The wife collects what she calls "Chinoiserie" and she says...'

He was interrupted by the return of Appleyard, his eyebrows contracted so that they made a straight line across his face. He was very angry.

'That damn girl. I knew she'd cause trouble.'

'Does she give us a lead?'

The superintendent snarled. 'More likely a blasted waste of good time. She's vanished, hopped off on some wildcat chase of her own, I should think. It seems that she didn't sleep in the house last night and no one noticed because no one was there to notice until quite late this morning, when the char or housekeeper or whatever turned up, a Mrs Hayes. She's a busybody of a woman – one of those who love making themselves important. "I'm responsible for the poor thing now her dad's away. She's been kidnapped, that's what. We're none of us safe in our own beds. She'd never have gone off without leaving a message. It's all terrible." Mrs Hayes cycled all the way to Orwell to tell us so.'

'Anything in it?'

'The girl's up to something, no doubt of that. Her car's missing from the house but she doesn't seem to have taken anything with her – pyjamas or whatever kids wear nowadays if they don't sleep naked. No toothbrush or washing things.'

'A dirty night with a boy-friend?'

Appleyard had hunched his shoulders.

'It doesn't fit my idea of that little madam. If she hasn't turned up by tonight then she's deeper in this than I can figure right now. Meantime I've put out an inquiry for the lady. I want her for a nice long cosy chat.'

7

The Oncer

'She's gone.'

Smith, R.O., sitting gloomily beside Mr Campion on a patch of scrawny grass, hit out at the nettles within his reach, decapitating them with a switch he had cut from the undergrowth with his newly restored knife.

'She's gone,' he repeated. 'She didn't mean to go, because she told me. I don't like it. Would you?'

'You had a date with her?'

'Sort of. She didn't turn up at the dig when she said she would and she's always bang on time. Mrs Hayes, the caretaker at Peregrine's, was raising hell there when I looked in. She's run screaming off to the police. At least she's done something about it which is more than I have. What the hell do you think I ought to do?'

'I think,' said Mr Campion judicially, 'that you should tell me your full name, to complete the formal introduction, and if she doesn't reappear you should come into Brett village with me this evening and see if the Mainsail's Yachtsman's grill is any good.

Ever tried it?'

The young man considered the proposition. Now that he had confided his anxieties he found them increasing and the possibility of action seemed infuriatingly remote. But this vague spectacled stranger was interested enough to take him seriously and, moreover, seemed to have some direct connection with the problem. At least he was worth cautious cultivation.

'Decent of you. If she's not here by six – that's when they knock off at the dig and she's bound to come over if she's back – I'd like to feed with you.' He grinned. 'My name is Robert Oncer Smith and my crew call me Oncer. Don't make wisecracks about "once is enough" – I've heard them all.'

'Rely on me,' said Mr Campion. 'I have one Christian name that I don't admit even to myself.'

Having accepted hospitality, Mr Smith became an informed guide. 'If you go for this sort of jazz,' he said, 'the dig has got something. We've worked out the lines of the hull and some of our lot are making a scale model. We're still a bit doubtful about the upper-works but they seem to follow the general layout shown on some of the carvings from Ostia. The trouble is they're wildly inaccurate – the artists weren't seafaring types.'

He led Mr Campion along the edge of the excavated through to the long wooden hutment, sought permission from authority to enter and gave his mind to the tour.

The walls were covered with a patchwork of photographs and paper cuttings pinned haphazard: Roman bas reliefs, sectional drawings of archaic shipping and prints from the nautical museums of the world competed with the work of an amateur cartoonist, and across a noticeboard intended for announcements of duty rosters a strip of paper had been pinned with the words *'Avez-vous de la ferraille?'* neatly scripted.

Two trestle tables took up the centre of the room. On the first, new discoveries were being catalogued and collated by a bearded youth aided by twittering female acolytes speaking knowledgeable jargon.

'A thole, darling? Be your age. The cleats are too far apart even for Nydam style. Dream up something...'

The second table was devoted to pottery. Here there were places for six workers but only a single earnest lady toiled silently, piecing together fragments of what had once been a two-handled amphora. A complete example hung from the roof in front of her and opposite the empty positions other wine containers in varying sizes and designs were suspended. Beneath them were trays containing numbered fragments.

'Commander King's idea,' explained the guide in a respectful whisper. 'The hanging urns are borrowed, so that we can see what we're aiming at – what the broken stuff was like when it started life. Most of them don't stand up by themselves – I suppose they fitted into holders when they weren't in use. This way if you get a piece of odd pot you can try round and see what part it came from once you've spotted the original design. Our chaps have rebuilt about a dozen already.'

'I was told about a gold coin,' murmured Mr Campion. 'Diocletian, I think. Were many found?'

'Not a lot so far – six or seven. Out of the Skipper's private chest perhaps. We think it was a cargo ship probably bringing wine across the channel. Rather like our own *Sam Pepys*, only more upper-works. Old Matty said he thought she sank when she was anchored off-shore with the crew on leave. Sabotage by the local resistance movement perhaps. No skeletons or fragments of bone, you see. It went slap down into quick mud. Then there was a small earthquake. They've had quite a few in these parts – the last was only about eighty years ago and the river changed course. There's something about the soil here, if I could remember old Matty's bafflegab, that preserves things rather well. It also tells you where some of them are. Anything silver turns it purple, so you know where to look.'

Mr Campion was properly impressed.

'What happens to the valuable stuff?' he inquired. 'Not kept here, surely?'

Oncer shrugged his shoulders. Having done his duty his mind had returned to more pressing problems.

'At the Orwell Museum for vetting and restoring, I think. There isn't much, so far. A couple of swords and a thing called a standard-iron with a wolf standing on a hoop and some silver tops of drinking mugs. Does this sort of thing really ring bells with you? It did with old Matty. He used to do his nut when we found anything good.'

'I like to live and learn,' said Mr Campion quietly. 'You never know when an odd fact may come in handy – the co-efficient of the expansion of copper or who made Lord Beaconsfield's corsets. Or indeed, when they start serving dinner at your local.'

By seven o'clock the Mainsail, a white weatherboarded house which leaned comfortably upon itself and its neighbours, was beginning to fill up with the custom which it attracted from holiday sailors. It faced the river above a broad stone-flagged walk and the dining-room looked out on a jungle of small craft whose masts made black verticals against an overbright sky.

Mr Campion parked his car in the yard behind the hostelry and spent some time examining the other occupants of the cobbled square. He seemed in no hurry and gave no

95

indication that he had found what he was looking for. Finally he dispatched his unhappy companion to the bar with instructions to order a preliminary drink and to ensure a table by the window.

The meal, a modest affair of steak and chips, was not a social success. The young man was willing enough to talk about the school and its archaeological discovery but his mind was not on either topic. Despite gentle prodding from his host he lapsed into uneasy silence.

Mr Campion tried a new tack. 'Tell me about Mr Matthews,' he said. 'You knew him pretty well. Could you describe him?'

'Old Matty?' Oncer Smith was relieved to be given a chance to show he could behave as a polite guest should. He closed his eyes and selected his words.

'Yes,' he said after a pause. 'Yes, I can. He was a pretty vivid type – you wouldn't forget him. I mean, he had a sort of air about him as if he were one of those personalities who are bosses in their own line, or as if he was famous and didn't really care a damn for anybody. He knew a hell of a lot about anything he talked about – ships, for example, or odd spots abroad. I think he'd been all over the world. He knew about tides and currents and weather and earthquakes and deep-sea diving, though I don't think he was a sailor. He could make you laugh by debunking a bit of pomp with a few well-chosen words and he got up the snouts of one or two of the masters here when they were chucking their weight about at the dig. Commander King was glad of his help but he hated his guts all the same.'

He broke off and turned directly to the older man. 'Didn't you know him? You had my penknife which he'd borrowed. He was terribly sorry about it because he thought he'd lost it and bought me another one. I didn't really want it – the old one, I mean – because it's mostly a lot of useless junk and the blades weren't much good.'

Mr Campion hedged diplomatically.

'As I said, I came by it quite honestly. It was given to me to return to the rightful owner. Mission accomplished. What did he look like?'

'Oh, tallish – taller than me anyhow and I'm six feet. He had a bit of a stoop and a lot of grey hair which he never brushed, or not much anyway. A craggy sort of face, beaky, you know, weather-beaten, and those rather crinkled eyes you get if you live a lot in the sun – most naval types have them. As for age, I'm no sort of judge. Sometimes he behaved like a chap in the lower fourth. Foggy Peregrine's going to retire next year, which makes him around sixty, I suppose. He was that sort of make-up – only much fitter. Or at least we all thought he was.' Regret clouded his face. 'Do you get the picture?'

'Perfectly,' said Mr Campion. 'You haven't got a snap of him by any chance?'

His guest smiled for the first time that evening.

'Funny you should say that. Matty wouldn't join in any of the dreary group photographs that people always want to take. You know – "The team that found the old iron pot" – "Professor Burp with merry helpers at work" – all that jazz. He just wouldn't play. There's no proper official one of him but young Bourchier – he's what we call a mid and a very low form of life – was always messing around with his second-hand Leica. He took dozens, mostly lousy, but there was one of Matty, I remember. He was with a lot of chaps and laughing like a drain because they'd just unearthed a Roman spanner which had "Singer Sewing Machine Co." stamped on it.'

'Do you think you could raise a print for me?'

'Bourchier's on leave, of course – summer holidays to you. If he's left any stuff here it would be in his locker, which is a bit private even if he is a dreary little wet.'

'A pity.'

'Is it all that urgent? I mean, would it help about this trouble?'

'It might,' said Mr Campion. 'It might be the key to the whole mystery.'

Oncer was in no mood for inaction. He had found the long silences embarrassing and the opportunity to do something immediate was attractive.

'There's a chance,' he said. 'A bit of a long shot and it could take all night, but Bourchier may have left some of his stuff in the school dark room. Lots of people do. It's a room off the physics lab and there are thousands of bad prints and old negs lying about all over the place. It's like a washhouse, all strings and clips holding chunks of film. It's supposed to be cleaned up at the end of term but I doubt if it has been, knowing Bourchier and his gang of squirts. We could try it.'

'You can get in without being spotted?'

'Nothing simpler. I've known every trick for getting in and out of Brett for donkey's years – ever since I first broke bounds for a hot grog and shag party in my second year. And I wasn't sick either.' He pushed back his chair. 'Shall we go?'

Mr Campion looked at his watch, 'I'd like to come with you but I don't want to attract awkward questions,' he said. 'The best time for breaking and entering is after dark. If you agree I think we should behave professionally. Burglary is a very serious business.'

The Brett school by starlight was a place of unearthly beauty. Slates glimmered like scales on a sleeping dragon and the buildings beneath them crouched in formal patterns, black and white, softened by the enchantment of beckoning detail which defied recognition. Samuel Pepys, presiding over the forecourt from his plinth guarded by the barrels of cannon captured by Nelson, linked with anchor chains, saw nothing of the night's enterprise.

Oncer Smith had his own peculiarly informed method of approach. He halted Mr Campion at the head of the lime avenue which led to the forecourt and made a personal reconnaissance of the porter's lodging.

'The policeman's cycle is parked at the gate,' he whispered. 'That means he's inside with old Gamage. In term time they sometimes do a late tour together and that can be tricky. They're probably waiting to see if Anthea turns up – she'd have to come down the avenue. All clear so far.'

He led the way by a series of shrubberies following a route which had clearly been established over the years by the more adventurous sons of Brett, indicating their position as they moved. 'We're at the back of the maths school now. The Head's house and Peregrine's are away on the left. Science block straight ahead. We go in by the coal hole – six steps down and the padlock pulls out of the door complete.'

Beyond the black heaps of fuel there was a second door unlatched and a few inches ajar. Mr Campion produced a torch to reveal a boiler-room, a cavernous area of mysterious pipes, stacked shovels, packing-cases, old motor tyres, drums of paint and oil and a table on which stood an empty beer bottle, a pile of dogeared magazines and two packs of cards. A stone staircase in the far corner led upwards into darkness.

'The old secret glory hole – still used by the kids, you see. It's a piece of cake from now on. The lab is on the first floor. Let's go.'

Mr Campion held out the torch. 'Shine it on the ground if you have to use it and keep a handkerchief over it. Do you still talk about keeping *cave?* I propose to do just that from the comfort of this bench. I can't help in the dark room and you know the layout. Good luck.'

Oncer was not pleased. 'If I'm caught I can probably talk myself out of it. You'll be for the high jump if you're alone. We're better together.'

The older man's whisper became imperative, 'I'm running this piece of larceny. If you want to be useful you'll have to take orders. Leave all the doors wide as you go and keep an ear cocked for any trouble. If I want to warn you I'll kick over a shovel or upset a pile of oil drums. If that happens, then get out some other way. This isn't the time for rocking the boat. Understood?'

'Understood.'

It was some time after the last flicker of

the torch had vanished before Mr Campion's eyes became attuned to the darkness. He took off his spectacles and his jacket, placed them on the table, listened for a moment at the door to the coal hole and then began clearing a space on the boiler room side of it, exploring the floor with a cautious foot to make certain that nothing remained to cause an incriminating sound.

Far off in the forecourt the bell clock struck the half-hour: the echoes dwindled and died leaving a void as arid as blotting paper. The familiar brackish scent of acid from a century of schoolboy experiments in chemistry floated into the room on a draught of air, infiltrating the closer reek of stale water heated and cooled in ancient pipes. Oncer had reached his destination and was following instructions. Mr Campion waited, his back to the wall beside the door. It was a long vigil, silent and featureless.

Without warning a pencil of light from a second torch appeared from the doorway, explored the room and vanished, making the gloom momentarily blinding. Very close to him, inside the room now, someone was breathing, the quick shallow intake that goes with a heart beating too fast. A minute passed before the light reappeared and in the first instant Mr Campion jumped from behind, gripping the dark figure round the neck and twisting the arm which held the torch so that it fell to the ground and vanished. The scuffle was surprisingly short.

'If you try anything funny, Mr Ginger Scott, you'll find yourself with a broken arm. I hope I make myself clear?'

'For Chrissake ... you've done it already. Let up, will you? Ye're killing me.' The thin voice out of the blackness had south London and Glasgow dispiritingly mingled. 'Ye're killing me,' it repeated. 'Lemme breathe or I'll spew ma guts out.'

Mr Campion confirmed his grip with a twist which brought a whimper of genuine pain.

'Listen carefully, Ginger, or I'll turn you in. You wouldn't care for that, would you, after the lecture you got this morning? Breaking and entering, you know. Too bad with a record like yours. Another of the best years of your life gone to waste. Do you want to talk?'

'I don't want nothing. Ease up or I'll die on you.'

'Who sent you here, Ginger? I can wait all night for the answer, but you won't care for the experience.'

'I don't know. If you were Gawdalmighty I couldn't say. I don't know ... you're breaking my arm.'

Mr Campion was aware of a new odour, a compound of sweat, hair cream and terror but he did not relax.

'We'll begin at the beginning, then. Who

pays you? Or are you doing it for fun?'

'I don't know. For Chrissake I don't...'The voice wavered, choked into a whisper. 'Okay then, but it won't help you. It's not my fault if I can't grass, is it? I was put on this lark by Wilkie Collins – they call him that, see? – a con man I met in the Scrubs. He's a fixer and a right bastard. I wouldn't touch him except he passed me on and staked me. Not his money, not his lark, whatever it is. Just a fixer.'

'But you get orders. You have to report – to let somebody know exactly what I'm doing. For three days now you've been following me. Who do you talk to?'

'I don't know. It's God's truth, that is. I'd split if I knew. I swear to you...'

Mr Campion lowered the pinioned arm by a fraction 'You talk to someone by radio, a little walkie-talkie set, don't you? I found it in your car this evening where you left it in the yard of the Mainsail. Very careless – it's the way to lose valuable property. It's extremely short range, so you must know where to be at certain times.'

'Right. I'm spilling all I can. I'm trying to help, see? I'm talking. O.K., O.K., so I get letters, letters and cash. I'm told where to go, what time to be waiting.'

'And a call signal?'

'Come again?'

'When your buzzer goes, you don't just say

104

"Scott here", or do you? Anyone can pick up short-wave radio if they happen to be on the wavelength. How do they know it's you? You'd better speak up or I may have to do a little talking myself. The call signal, remember?'

'When they want me, they say "A message for MacTavish" and I say "It's no the Mac-Tavish, but the MacDonald".'

'And you talk in clear? No code words?'

'No code at all. Can I go now for Gawd's sake? I swear I'll not trouble you. Never ... so long as I live...'

Mr Campion frog-marched the twisted figure to the door of the coal hole.

'Now run for it,' he said.

He returned to the boiler-room to find Oncer descending the steps, his torch glowing discreetly.

'Any luck?'

'Bags of it. I found three pegs and I'm pretty sure Matty's in all of them, though in one his back is turned. I say, I thought I heard voices. Did you have trouble?'

'No trouble at all,' said Mr Campion.

8

Unfinished Business

The upper floors of Omega House are said to command all the finest views of London and the city itself cannot escape an equally clear vision of Omega House. The exchange is imperfectly balanced, for the enormous column of concrete and glass known as the Oildrum is uncompromising and undistinguished.

The room on the executive floor marked 'Management (W)' housed L.C. Corkran in chromium magnificence but it did not please him despite his efforts to humanize it. His Pisarro, a wet autumnal sketch of the Place Blanche, was too small for the background and the walnut bookcase containing his more favoured classics appeared to be waiting removal to some happier setting. Outside, and far below, from the dome of St Paul's via the rectangular newcomers hiding the river to the figure of Justice over the Old Bailey, the panorama had the remote unreality of an aerial view.

On his desk three enlarged prints, blown to the limit the grain would allow, lay side by side. Corkran picked up each in turn, replacing them as if he had some meticulous pattern in mind and accuracy was essential.

'I'm afraid,' he said, 'that this is conclusive. I only met the man once, and briefly at that. But I have no doubts.'

Mr Campion sighed. His chair was too low for comfort and he stood up, straightening his spectacles.

'It can be confirmed?'

'At once.' Corkran pressed a button. 'Mrs Devenish, can you spare me a minute or two?'

The woman who appeared through an inner door was plump as a pullet and as unimpressive as a piece of bad knitting. Only her eyes betrayed efficiency. She waddled comfortably to Corkran's side of the desk and looked down on the display.

'Well?'

'It's Francis Makepeace. No mistaking him with a face like that. If you want details, the wrinkle above his nose is slightly irregular owing to a scar. It shows clearly on the centre print. His nose has four or five hairs growing just above the bridge and I see he hasn't dealt with them yet. As for the back of his head – well, he always needed a good haircut and I've often told him about it. So you've found him?'

'I'm afraid so,' said Corkran dryly. 'No action yet, Mrs Devenish. We lack a few

107

details. Will you take these for filing?'

When her departure had restored the modernity to the room he nodded towards the door.

'Better than any computer that was ever designed, you know. She's been here so long that she has what you might call tribal memory. Poor Makepeace. A pity to pry into his secret. It was *odi profanum vulgus et arceo* after all. One can hardly blame him for wanting to escape. I've been wasting your time, Albert, on something that wasn't worth powder and shot. I'm sorry.'

'You said we lack a few details.' Mr Campion was apologetic. 'Major details, I would call them, if you'll forgive me. A lot of awkward facts refuse to fit into your pigeon-hole. Makepeace – my Mr Matthews – was up to something before he died, something that needed more than ordinary secrecy. It could be that he was thinking of selling out on you, but you have dismissed that as out of character and after talking to one or two of his friends I'm inclined to agree. Makepeace alive might be an attractive proposition to any of your competitors but why the interest in Makepeace dead? Is he likely to have put anything on paper?'

Corkran raised an eyebrow, rubbed his nose with a bony forefinger and swivelled in his top executive chair. It was some time before he spoke.

'The answer must be no. It was very difficult to get him to write anything at all. His minutes or memoranda, when he was forced into producing them, were inclined to be brief, pointed and rude – schoolboy rude when he considered them unnecessary. The idea that he might have marked up maps in detail – development areas for example – is naïve and ridiculous. He was concerned with large-scale policy decisions and all those he carried in his head. He didn't need paper to betray secrets. Half an hour with his opposite number in any rival enterprise would be quite enough.'

'Yet his property has attracted a lot of attention. A man who showed interest in it – the hotel manager who had a reputation for curiosity – lost his life whilst playing Paul Pry in Matthews's cottage, or so the police think. The girl who owns the place, and probably was closer to him than anyone else, has vanished. The local police are very cagey about admitting this because the lady has an independent nature and, I gather, a sharpish tongue. At least two sets of people excluding myself have been asking questions about the late Mr Matthews. It goes a trifle beyond the minor detail category wouldn't you say?'

Corkran was discomforted. He disliked the presentation of flaws in an argument which he had hoped was closed. He was a tidy man.

'As you present the case, I admit it is

thoroughly unsatisfactory. How far do you think it concerns us – what proportion, if any, is attributable to the fact that he had valuable information? The man appears to have had some animal instinct to escape, to be private. It might arouse the cupidity of small pre-dators.'

'Rather big ones, I'm afraid,' said Mr Campion diffidently. 'I smell a lot of money being spent on research into Makepeace and his activities. I think there are figures in the background who ought to be identified before you can close your file.'

'In fact, you want to continue?'

'In fact, I intend to. I have a personal interest in the matter now – a Mr Smith, whom I wish well, and his missing girl-friend, Miss Peregrine.'

Corkran conceded defeat. He admitted to himself that the problem still existed and could not be shelved but he gave way with-out enthusiasm. He shrugged his shoulders and pulled a sheet of paper from under his blotter.

'In that case,' he said, 'I think you should read this. You asked for some very short wave monitoring to be done in the area between Great Burdon and Orwell. A very wide belt of country. It has been an expensive job, using a lot of personnel and their time has been largely wasted. They have eliminated everything that is not on the precise wavelength you gave me and anything obviously irrelevant. But they have come up with some results. Among others a message for your friend MacTavish. My man gave the response you indicated and acknowledged some instructions in the absence of the rightful recipient. What happened to him by the way?'

'His set was stolen.' said Mr Campion. 'Without it he has no ears and no mouth. I'm afraid he may have lost interest by now. He was a very unstable type – careless with valuable equipment. May I?'

He held out his hand for the typescript and began to read:

Messages recorded from short-range transmitter within three miles of Great Burdon, Oxon, between 6.30 p.m. and 7 p.m. Aug. 14th. No other transmissions were made on this wavelength during the period Aug. 13 noon to Aug. 15 noon. Speaker was male apparently reading from prepared script. Gist of messages only is given, not full transcript.

(1) To Barney's Bull. (Response: 'Not Barney's but O'Reilly's.') Still unsatisfactory. The source is not the one required. Try again but not through anyone already known to you. 5,000 (?£5,000) limit.

(2) To the Angel Gabriel. (Response: 'Not Gabriel but Michael.') O seven two not O seven three. This cannot be a coincidence. Follow up

111

and report urgently.

(3) To Honest John. (Response: 'Not Honest but Willing.') Get the name of the firm through the clerk. Pay for this information. Then go ahead and travel if necessary.

(4) To the MacTavish. (Response as instructed.) Walk slowly down the steep path from the Stone on Thursday evening starting 8 p.m.

Mr Campion looked up to find his old friend eyeing him with a wry smile. Like many an academic, Corkran concealed his envy for the man who was not tied to an office.

'Stone?' he inquired. 'I take it the name has some significance for you?'

'The Stone of Burdon – a prehistoric monolith. Hence the name Great Burdon. It stands a mile or so out of the village and it should be a landmark but it happens to have fallen down. There's been trouble about setting it up again ever since Humpty Dumpty fell off his wall. All the King's horses couldn't do the job and now it is a matter for the Office of Works. *"Burdon's Stone has fallen down Burdon men have no renown Raise it up without delay Burdon girls come out to play."* That's how the song goes, with a great many more verses and most of them splendidly earthy. You don't know the ditty?'

'My education is incomplete,' said Corkran primly. *'Non omnia possumus omnes.* If

112

you're keeping that rendezvous I think it would be wise if I provided some cover for you. A couple of men at a respectable distance, perhaps?'

Mr Campion shook his head.

'Alone, I think. I'd like the conversation to be uninhibited.'

9

Rendezvous

Mr Campion reached the Great Stone of Burdon after the sun had left a limpid sky flecked with gilded specks of cloud. From the main road a worn track across common land was fringed on the southern side by trees, the outposts of Burdon forest. The Stone, invisible from a distance, was indicated by a board bearing the inscription 'Celtic Monument. *Circa* 1300 B.C.'

It lay like the abandoned coffin of a thirty-foot giant pointing due west, surrounded by trodden earth, reinforced with cinders made tawdry by the cartons and debris of sight-seers, for the view across the Cotswold Hills was broad and gracious. Beyond, the ground sloped sharply downwards and though the footpath was visible it did not enjoy the popularity of the easier track from the road.

At eight precisely Mr Campion, armed with binoculars and a shooting-stick, began the descent, keeping to the track which led towards a level area of bushes, coarse grass and saplings before pausing in a belt of self-seeded larches.

Ahead of him a dark mass took shape, resolving itself into the figure of a man sitting on a folded canvas chair with a tartan rug over his knees. Above him a large green painter's umbrella on a pole stuck into the ground was fixed at an angle apparently to give protection against the evening wind. A wide-brimmed black hat hid most of his face. Beside him an Alsatian dog squatted on its haunches with ears pricked, imperiously drawing attention to the approaching stranger.

Mr Campion advanced at a casual pace and halted in front of the group. The dog snarled and was stilled by a gesture from its master.

'I'm afraid Mr Ginger Scott has abandoned his appointment. May I replace him?'

The man raised his head very slightly, his face a white blur behind tinted spectacles.

'You may if you stand perfectly still. My dog is unused to strangers and he is but lightly tethered. He has a nervous temperament, you may say a mischievous one – perhaps cruel would be a better word. At times I am unable to control him.'

He cleared his throat in a rattling wheeze and leaned forward, his hands clasped over the handle of his stick.

'Now, sir, you have intruded upon me, and by intention – that is evident. This is a public place and I cannot prevent such be-

115

haviour. You may say that you are replacing a man you name as Scott. Therefore you know something of him, you are acquainted or have encountered him. You are tall, enviably thin, bespectacled and speak with the accent of education. By inference, by logical deduction, your name is Campion. You fit every description I have received. I may take it that I am correct?'

'You may. Would your dog object if I were to sit?'

'By all means open your shooting-stick. It will make it difficult to use as a weapon of defence or offence. Now, Mr Campion, you are intervening in my affairs and that is a gesture which I find impertinent – not to be tolerated without explanation. I am intolerant by nature and that condition is exacerbated by my health. Do you offer me an explanation?'

The thin man settled himself with as much comfort as the device permitted.

'I would have thought,' he said mildly, 'that you have a lopsided view of the position. I proceed upon my lawful occasions, causing no trouble that I can see, and I find myself being spied on, very efficiently, by a small-time crook evidently acting on your instructions. A little research leads me to this unlikely rendezvous. Could you bring yourself to look at it in that light?'

The figure in the chair did not respond for some time. He snapped a finger at the dog which drew closer and allowed the back of its ears to be fondled.

'That is a conceivable position. I admit it but I do not accept it. My interests must take priority – they are paramount, not to be questioned. Yours I do not entirely understand. My information is that you are a man of some substance, with the reputation of a busybody, a dilettante adventurer.' He paused to breathe deeply, pursing his lips as he exhaled. 'I am not prepared to be frank with you – I am secretive by nature and by reason of my business. But my name is Porteous, Claude Porteous, which is no secret. It would be ridiculous to make the attempt since my appearance is memorable – repellent you may say. I cannot escape it – it is a prison without a door. It seems that we have a common interest – the activities of the late Matthew James Matthews. Can you enlighten me, or am I to regard you as an opponent – an obstacle which will have to be removed or circumnavigated?'

Mr Campion raised his eyebrows.

'At the moment,' he said, 'I should describe that as a pretty poor bargain. I tell you every card in my hand in return for which you refrain from giving me the treatment which was handed out to a man called Newgate who was also trying to investigate the late Mr Matthews. I think you should try a more tactful approach.'

117

Porteous raised his head so that his hidden eyes were unmistakably staring directly at Campion. The sudden movement brought a growl from the dog.

'I am unused to being treated flippantly. You make an accusation which you cannot possibly substantiate and suggest that I should be tactful. That is stupid – it lacks logic – it wastes my time and yours.

'You ask for a different approach. Very well, then. I am perfectly prepared to pay for information – there is no other means at my disposal. It seems probable that you have at least a part of the intelligence I need. I shall put it to you without hypocrisy, without ornament. Do you want to be paid to answer my questions?'

'A handsome bribe, I hope? You said that Barney's Bull could go up to five thousand.'

The wheezy voice gave no indication of surprise. 'So you have been eavesdropping by means of radio? I should have appreciated that. It was self-evident but the point escaped me. My methods of communication may be theatrical but in general they are functional – they amuse me and I have very few pleasures. The greater part, the vast majority, of my transactions are unquestionably legal. That is a necessity, not a virtue. There is no morality in my business, simply practical consideration. It is only when I meet subterfuge, trickery or obstinacy – elements which I try to eliminate, to avoid – that I am forced into using a certain type of undesirable lackey. I employ unlikely tools when I am obliged to, occasionally inefficient ones, who might talk too much when I no longer have use for them. It is better that they should have an improbable tale to tell. Who, for example, would believe your story if you said that you had encountered, by an appointment which you had intercepted out of the air, a fat stranger sitting under an umbrella protected by a vicious hound in open country two miles from the nearest house? And that you had talked to him of murder, accused him of it by inference, and suggested that you were interested in bribery? It is moonshine and melodrama, not to be credited. You must agree to that – no other description is conceivable.

'I have no wish to be personal with you, sir, but I admit to behaving as I do to please myself. I must have compensations for my cumbersome body, which is a curse to me. To behave like a creature from a gothic fantasy is one of them. I enjoy it and it has the advantage of making my detractors sound insane.'

A forefinger, lifted imperatively, showed that he had paused only to recover breath.

'As to bribery. I think it improbable that I could approach you directly, that is with money – with currency. My disposition is not generous and I would require information

119

which I could use, not theories or guesses. Facts – indisputable truths in answer to my questions. No concealment – nothing withheld. In return I could give you, for example, a sketch by Goya or Guardi. A trinket for your wife or your mistress? A trifle of that nature is difficult to trace and is not immediately suspect. Do I have your attention?'

Mr Campion resettled his shooting-stick.

'Very handsome indeed. But Matthews is dead. If he possessed something you wanted why approach me? Why not his heirs?'

'Because I am not satisfied that they exist. I am not satisfied that Matthews existed. Do not mistake me, sir. Certainly, a man is dead – the man known by that name in Great Burdon is dead – a natural death, quite unexpected, except by those who can read the warrant on a man's face. But there are indications that he was not what he pretended to be, that he had changed his identity, and possibly his appearance too. That is the mystery I intend to solve and I do not contemplate being frustrated, even if there are others – yourself included – who are acting in rivalry.

'Do you have anything to contribute, enough to justify my offer, or am I wasting my time?'

The light was beginning to lose the false brilliance which follows sundown and the dog pricked its ears, holding its head on one side to watch a paper bag as it scuttled past, propelled by an erratic breeze.

'Until I know what your business with Matthews was,' said Mr Campion. 'I shall not be in a helpful mood.'

The statement seemed to surprise the man in the chair. He lifted his stick and drove the ferrule deeply into the ground.

'I am not a dealer in penny packets, sir,' he said at last. 'You should have deduced that by now. Matthews was, because he was an amateur. In my opinion he was experimenting, learning the tricks of the trade. A hard man of some shrewdness according to my information, who was rapidly becoming adept – adroit. That suggested to me – and the idea was implemented by the man himself – that he had something very much larger in mind, something that could interfere with or upset the whole business which engages me.

'The thought disturbed me – it impaired my digestion, my health. I decided to make a personal investigation to observe what I could with my own eyes. If I was satisfied that he was a principal I intended a personal touch. His death forestalled me. Does that answer your question?'

'An amateur?' inquired Mr Campion mildly. 'An odd description, I would have thought.'

Porteous drew a long husky breath before he replied.

'An amateur in matters of money,' he said at last. 'Astute enough when it came to making a bargain, a commonplace deal – there is no question of that. He did not foresee the consequences, the disruption that could follow if he moved in the direction I suspected.

'Big interests must be protected against any ignoramus who does not understand money. It is a commodity which needs a great deal of understanding. It is a force – it must be used as water is used to turn a dynamo. If it is sluggish it must be directed into channels, it must be dammed until it becomes a torrent which can be translated into power. The man Matthews had information, dynamite which could blow a hole in the banks of such a stream – a little hole which was valuable to him, no doubt, but in the ultimate could prove disastrous, catastrophic.

'I intend to prevent such an occurrence and I shall not be nice or over-scrupulous in my methods if I think it necessary. Morality is a myth, a superstition, in the face of larger considerations.

'Let me give you a trivial example to underline my meaning. My dog is trained to be ferocious, to display a brutality beyond his nature. Upon instruction he would savage a man, possibly kill him if he himself was counter-attacked. From time to time he has been condemned to death by the authorities

122

for his exploits but he is too valuable for such treatment. An animal resembling him is therefore handed to the official executioner and the public conscience is satisfied.'

He broke off to clear his throat.

'If you do not follow my argument, Mr Campion, then you have fewer wits than your reputation suggests. I made you an offer because it is patent that you already know a great deal about Matthews and are seeking to know more. Do you want to continue the discussion?'

The thin man did not respond for some time. He lit a cigarette, returned the lighter to his pocket and finally spoke in the casual tone of a man who wishes to change the subject.

'Anthea Peregrine,' he said. 'Do you know the lady?'

Porteous lifted his head sharply but his rheumy voice gave no indication of surprise.

'I have encountered her. She has a mind of her own, remarkable, but not unique in a modern young woman. I would not hesitate to use her as a lever on you or anyone else if I thought the method would produce results. Unfortunately she has an independent spirit in addition to physical charm. She has elected not to co-operate and, as you are probably aware, she has disappeared.'

'Of her own volition?'

'That is my understanding. If I could enlighten you, I would do so, at a price. I don't offer bargains, Mr Campion, and I suspect those who do. I shall put it to you this way. Let us suppose that at this stage the total cash value of the venture which engages me is six hundred thousand pounds. Not an exact figure, but serviceable, entirely credible, as you may or may not appreciate. Very well then, let us say that the puzzle, the jigsaw, has a hundred pieces. You, in my opinion, hold only one of them. Your contribution therefore, inescapably, logically, is worth six thousand pounds at its maximum. The gift I suggested to you, in whatever form it took, would have a re-sale value of around five thousand four hundred pounds. I am allowing a ten per cent margin for my private account, but if you were not greedy, were prepared to wait, you could recover the total, perhaps double it, within a twelve-month.'

The black cane between his hands had a tee-shaped ivory handle and he rocked it forward as if it were the major control of an aircraft.

'What can you tell me about Matthew James Matthews?'

Mr Campion stood up.

'Nothing at all, I'm afraid.' He folded the seat of the shooting stick and pulled the spike from the ground. 'By the way, your caravan, beyond the trees over there, is showing a light. If I were handling your publicity I would say that carelessness of that sort was bad for your image.'

The tinted glasses, now black caverns in a pale mass, gave the face the appearance of a death's head. The dog pricked its ears and whimpered.

'Your own bodyguard has been detected,' said Porteous. 'Someone is watching us from a safe distance. I respect that – I approve of reasonable caution. In case I am mistaken about his identity – his association with you – let me advise you. He is now in the group of silver birch trees behind you and has been creeping nearer to us for some time. I wish you good evening, Mr Campion.'

10

The Expert

The track leading up stiffly to the Stone was not easy to negotiate in the half light. Mr Campion climbed slowly, scrambling and tripping, pausing occasionally to listen; but the turf absorbed every foothold and it was only when he unfolded his stick and sat leaning his back against the Stone itself that he was certain that he was being followed.

The approaching stranger, a compact upright figure, silhouetted against the sky, made no effort at concealment and as he drew level the thin man wished him a polite 'Good evening'.

'Mr Campion?'

The voice had a suggestion of authority, the brusqueness of a policeman or a senior official.

'Keeping an eye on me?'

'My instructions were to do just that.'

A torch sprang to life in the man's hand and he played the beam unexpectedly upwards on himself, revealing a square head with a clipped moustache above a solid chin, an aggressive, slightly outdated face suggestive of a

126

pre-war regular officer.

'My name's Lampeter. Mr Corkran thought you might be heading into trouble. Were you?'

'It was educational rather than dramatic,' said Mr Campion thoughtfully. 'I suppose you can prove who you are?'

'I can.' A notecase appeared containing an Omega House pass complete with an uncomplimentary photograph. 'My job is Security though I'm in what is called the personal division. Just what Mr Corkran does I'm not quite sure, though I could make a guess. He has Director status – Top Brass stuff. I just do as I'm told.' He switched off the torch and took Campion by the arm.

'I think we'll get moving if you don't mind. I don't know that fat scarecrow with the dog – the man you were talking to – but as soon as you left he was joined by two other characters. Too dark to see who they were. D'you know what they're up to?'

'The fat man's name is Claude Porteous, or so he says. Not quite the bogus type he pretends to be. Like ourselves he is looking into the question of the late Matthew Matthews, but for different reasons, I gather. Have you ever heard of him?'

'He's not in oil,' Lampeter spoke without hesitation, 'whoever he is. I'll look into it and get the answers as soon as I'm clear with you. Shall we move off?'

Mr Campion sensed antagonism, the resentment of a professional towards an outsider who has been introduced by higher authority. Cautiously he attempted to find common ground. 'You know all about the Matthews–Makepeace problem?' he suggested.

Lampeter was striding out, one hand on Campion's elbow, moving a little faster than was comfortable. 'I've been running the inquiry from the Omega end, if that's what you mean, or perhaps I should say I have been until recently. For your information I've been right through the file on him – which I understand is more than you have – and I'm bang in the picture as far as he's concerned. I may even be a jump ahead of you.' He quickened his pace.

'Your car,' said Mr Campion mildly, 'must be somewhere quite near. Suppose we adjourn to Great Burdon? I've booked a room there and we might have a meal? A blasted heath is no place to talk shop.'

The pacemaker accepted the suggestion without grace. 'You can eat on me – my expense account isn't queried these days. And I'll drive with you if you don't mind. My chap can follow. I'm not looking for trouble. The idea is that I see you safely home.'

'It's a hard life being a nursemaid. I hope the Refectory at the Drover will provide compensations. With two expense accounts behind us we ought to find the best bottle in the cellar.'

They drove in silence and it was not until they were established at a banquet table in a corner of the half-empty dining-room that any true contact could be attempted. Lampeter remained uncompromisingly inside his shell, pretending an indifference to food but grudgingly admiring the choice of wine.

'Good stuff,' he said at last. 'It ought to be at that price. There was a Captain Chambertin with my lot, in my army days. No relation. I took the trouble to ask him.'

'You were in the S.I.B.?'

'Seconded to Intelligence – criminal intelligence in point of fact. I started life as a Detective Constable C.I.D. It gave me a goodish background for the kind of work I do now. I'm blessed with a photographic memory – better than the scanners who look you over when you go into the big money rooms at Monte Carlo, and they're supposed to know every crook in two continents.'

'And do *you?*'

'No,' said Lampeter flatly, 'I don't. But I can recognize the senior staff of our rivals and their hangers-on, their women and their personal friends. Porteous, whoever he is, doesn't fit in there. I know who talks to who, and generally why. As for crooks, the blow-flies in that area, particularly con-men, I know most of the regulars and I have a nose for the rest. Oil seems to attract them. Money and oil together.'

'What do you smell hereabouts?'

The professional surveyed the room. Only a few late diners now remained, gourmets dealing knowledgeably with cognac or port, their ladies gossiping over the last glass of Yquem.

'That's the odd thing,' he said. 'Not a single oily boy or hanger-on in the entire cartload. The little dried-up chap in the window table with a wife who looks like a duchess – was one once, come to think of it – has done time for fraud, but that was just bad luck. They called his bluff at the wrong moment. The only character of real interest has just gone out of the room. I don't suppose you noticed him. A little dark man, fiftyish, with curly black hair and a long sad face like a sheep.'

Mr Campion perceived that he was going to receive a lesson in observations designed to show that he was surplus to establishment. He retreated behind his glasses, sipping thoughtfully at the burgundy.

'There's a Mr Morris Jay on the hotel register,' he ventured. 'An antique dealer, I believe. No doubt he has quite legitimate business here because this place is just one long street of antique shops. He figured in that paragraph which Makepeace thought was worth clipping and he was staying here on the night when Matthews died. There was a man in grey with a dark blue shirt and a copy of the *Financial Times,* who could fit the bill. Is that the one?'

Lampeter eyed his companion without affection but a tinge of respect was reflected in his tone. It was disappointing to discover that perhaps Corkran had made a shrewd choice after all. He dismissed the thought.

'It may be unimportant – a coincidence. We've checked and rechecked on Jay and there seems to be nothing wrong with him except that he's filthy rich and very modest living. There's money in antiques, I suppose, if you know how to buy, or how to fake. Do you think there's anything to it?'

'He often does business here, I gather,' said Mr Campion with proper humility. 'As you know, the place is full of junk shops. Tell me about Makepeace. You said you'd read the full dossier. Did you find anything useful between the lines? Any trace of a chip on the shoulder?'

Again the thought which Lampeter had attempted to dismiss flickered and vanished.

'Could be. He could be what you might call an angry old man. He had some tax trouble about ten years back and considered himself ill-used – tricked – which is exactly my own opinion. He was working abroad for considerable stretches of time, all over the place, never in England except for a few odd days and in the normal way he'd have been tax free. Some clever johnnie in the Inland Revenue or the Treasury found a clause in the act ambiguously worded under which they might catch him and decided to make a test case of it. It cost him a mint of money. There are always one or two bloody-minded eggheads in the Civil Service who enjoy that sort of thing without any thought of the personal harm they cause or the ill-will they build up in the public mind. Makepeace was pretty badly mauled – robbed, I'd say – and he resented it just as anyone else would. I suppose Corkran didn't think fit to mention it?'

'Perhaps it was too far back. If Makepeace was going to make some sort of gesture by way of getting even he'd have done it before now. That's the way L.C.'s mind worked, I imagine. He didn't really question the man's honesty with the firm or his loyalty to the country. Out of character, in his opinion...'

He hesitated, acutely aware that he was risking giving offence.

'I think,' he continued at last, 'that it was because he felt there was no routine answer to the problem that he persuaded an outsider like myself to poke his oar in. Would you agree?'

Lampeter was only partially soothed. He shrugged his shoulders and frowned at the glass in his hand.

'Resentment can grow like cancer. What

132

Makepeace could reveal about the workings of Omega is worth a packet of any competitor's money. Every man has a price if it's big enough. Yet there's no smell of oil and God knows I'm pretty well aware of it if it's within a mile of me. And another thing...'

'Yes?' Mr Campion was the most respectful of audiences.

'I know all my opposite numbers – mostly men like myself with either police or army experience. A very shrewd hardworking lot. One of them at least, the chap from Pan-World-United, has been on the prowl also looking for Makepeace. So he certainly hasn't been near them. Yet if the man was going to sell out, then Pan-World is the most likely bet. They're still looking, so he didn't go there. I know this because Bill Quince, the man from Pan, had an arrangement with the porter at Makepeace's flat to tip him off if he reappeared there after he'd vanished. It wouldn't surprise me if Quince hasn't the same understanding at his club with a servant, or even with a clerk at his bank. I made similar arrangements when the thing first blew up.'

He sat back in his chair, a square peg in a square hole, tolerably pleased with himself, and produced a tobacco-pouch.

'They can't object to a pipe at this hour. I suppose you'll be drinking something special in the way of brandy. I'll take a long

133

whisky and water myself.'

They drank for some time in silence. The company in the room, which was too large to be authentic despite its venerable décor, was reduced to their own table and two business-men arguing importantly in a far corner. An elderly waiter, who had clearly been encouraged to grow white side-whiskers to go with the black panelling, leaned by the door sur-reptitiously reading a paper, an activity which the late manager would never have tolerated.

'There's something else, isn't there?' Mr Campion's tone was hesitant. 'Do you feel inclined to discuss it?'

Lampeter blew smoke into the air and indulged himself in a private smile.

'You're right. I was saving it for a nightcap as you might say – something to make you think as you tuck yourself up in William Shakespeare's bed or wherever you're sleeping. I'm dossing in an attic called Adam Bede, whoever he was. Waiter!'

The old man jerked to attention, dropping the paper on to the chair at his side. He moved towards them slowly on outsize feet, flat and bedevilled with corns.

'The same again, gentlemen?'

'In a minute, my boy.' Lampeter was authoritative. 'Now, how long did you say you'd been here?'

'Five years sir. Before that I was at the Lygon Arms and before that...'

'Never mind. You knew Mr Matthews who died here not long ago. You remember him well?'

'A very kind gentleman. Not at all mean, like some guests are who aren't regulars.'

'Good. This afternoon I showed you a photograph of a friend of mine. Did you recognize him?'

The old man hesitated.

'It's like I told you, sir. I think I'd seen his face before but I couldn't put a name to him. With the regulars I always know what to expect, they're registered with me in a manner of speaking. A bottle of Beaune, a Guinness or two large ports, if you follow me. Some of them...'

'Then you're sure it wasn't a photograph of Mr Matthews?'

'Oh, no, sir. You could say there was a sort of general likeness – same age, same sort of hair, not very tidy. But it wasn't Mr Matthews. And my eyes are sharp for my time of life. I'm a pensioner, even if I don't look it. I only work here because I like company, being a widower and my grandson in Canada. No, it wasn't Mr Matthews. What can I get you, sir?'

'The same again and make them large ones. Well, Mr Campion, what do you say to that?'

The thin man sighed. He cupped the monstrous balloon glass in his hands and waited until the decorative ancient was out of earshot.

'Oh dear,' he said at last. 'I suppose that with an efficient investigator like yourself it was bound to be discovered. Like you, I've suspected something of the sort for a day or two. The only difference is that I had an unfair advantage. I got to the photograph first.'

Lampeter was irked. His news had not scored the direct hit he had hoped for and he was uncertain whether his companion had been a leap ahead or was too smooth altogether. He fought back.

'According to Somerset House,' he said, 'where they keep pretty complete records I understand, there was a Matthew James Matthews, born in Delhi in 1902 of British parents, a construction engineer who died in Nice in 1960. I started from there. Furthermore, if you go back far enough – which I did – you'll find that he once worked for Petroleum Bruxelloise, which is a subsidiary of Omega.

'I don't get flashes of inspiration, Mr Campion. I do it by routine checking which is damn dull and very hard work. You should try it sometime.'

Mr Campion accepted the rebuke. He smiled and raised his glass. 'If we were playing tennis,' he observed, 'I would say that was "vantage" Lampeter. At the moment I'm going to stick my neck out by offering a

136

thought in all humility – two, now I come to consider it.'

'Your service,' said Lampeter dryly.

'The first is that I feel convinced we ought to keep absolutely quiet about your researches – even with the redoubtable L.C. Corkran. We don't want to alarm the quarry.'

'You could be right. I'll think that one over, so call it a let. What's your second point?'

'The second is pure guesswork,' said Mr Campion diffidently. 'I'm in sad need of some expert routine checking. It might be worth while to find out if any other ex-employee of Omega has gone missing lately. Perhaps someone on the field side who retired about five or six years ago. Try the Forest Hill area for a start.'

For the first time Lampeter lowered his professional guard.

'I'll call that deuce, if it suits you,' he said.

11

Emergency Exit

By the time Mr Campion descended the
broad Tudor staircase of the Drover's Arms,
one of its few genuine architectural treasures,
his companion of the previous night had paid
his bill and set off presumably to fresh fields
of inquiry, leaving no farewell message.
Although it was still early the hum of vacuum
cleaners made the air vibrate with conscious
virtue, bringing an implied rebuke for sloth.
Mr Campion took his car to the spot where
he had left it the evening before and retraced
his footsteps past Burdon Stone to the scene
of his rendezvous and beyond it to where a
narrow lane ambled between the remaining
acres of Burdon Forest.

Here the imprint of a heavy vehicle had
bruised the verge and a smaller track
indicated that a car had been halted beside
it. Cigarette-ends lay on the trodden grass,
damp tea-leaves and coffee grounds indicated that Porteous and his staff had eaten
an alfresco meal. They had evidently left
soon after nightfall for the morning dew still
lay in the indentations and across one of the

ruts a spider had woven a revealing trap.

By way of the hamlet of Little Burdon and the twin villages called the Penuries he returned to the Drover to find that the Ostler's Bar, festooned with horse brass and heraldry, was enjoying considerable patronage.

As he passed through the hall a man sitting alone raised his head sharply, a gesture which had been caught by a second figure standing just inside the bar room, a stranger who appraised him in a quick sidelong glance and turned away. The infection of curiosity had been conjured into the air and as it spread Mr Campion was aware that he had made one of his rare failures to achieve an inconspicuous entrance.

The Ostler's Bar was a place of deliberately dim nooks and corners, gate-legged tables and oaken settles, cunningly arranged to make the room appear a great deal smaller than in fact it was.

He found a space at the counter between the noonday imbibers and ordered a gin and tonic, waiting placidly for the ripples he had caused to subside. Despite the predictable nature of the guests who appeared to be divided evenly between Cotswold tourists and the comfortably padded middle English of the neighbourhood awaiting the arrival of their womenfolk from shopping expeditions, he was acutely aware that he was still under observation.

In the farthest alcove, his face obscured by the winged curve of the side of a built-in bench, a man in a blue shirt was talking earnestly to a girl with her back towards the room. Her hair was covered by a bright orange scarf and she was sitting straight and still, listening.

Mr Morris Jay had something which was both private and important to say. He was not expressing an opinion but stating something which he evidently regarded as absolute and his audience was giving him unwavering attention.

On an impulse Mr Campion swung round to find himself looking straight into the eyes of Robert Oncer Smith who was standing directly behind him. There was a perceptible pause before the young man acknowledged the encounter. Beneath his tan he blushed.

'I thought it was you,' he said. He lifted an empty glass halfway to his mouth, noticed the mistake and placed it on the counter.

'Have a drink. Please. I owe you one.'

Mr Campion accepted the offer.

'No deception. I just happen to be staying in the pub. And by the same token you just happen to be drinking here. Nothing to worry about. Cheer up, my dear chap. Your secret is safe with me.'

Oncer grinned an embarrassed acceptance of the inevitable, mingled with unspoken thanks for comfort in times past. His hands had become clumsy and his reply was a mumble just above a whisper.

'She's over there – Anthea, I mean. You spotted her, I expect, because I saw you looking that way. No one could miss her. She telephoned me the day after she went adrift and I came out to join her. Everything's O.K. now. I don't want to talk about it, if you don't mind.'

'Then I assume that you've seen an old friend whose death has been greatly exaggerated? When did you meet?'

The arrival of refreshment held up the conversation and Oncer made no effort to continue it. He poured the half-pint of bitter down his throat as if he was performing for a challenge, put down the glass and drew breath.

'I don't want to talk about it. That's what I said and I mean it. You were very decent to me when I was going round the bend. In return I did something for you, something I wouldn't have done if I'd known as much as I do now. Could we call it quits? If you must know, I've told Anthea all about you and you're the last person she wants to talk to. She said so herself. I'm sorry, but that's the way it is.'

'A pity,' said Mr Campion regretfully, 'a very great pity indeed. Since I'm not going to meet Miss Peregrine I wonder if you'd give her a message when she's free?'

'Anything you like. She may not take any notice but then she's got a mind of her own.'

The thin man glanced over his shoulder. Miss Peregrine had picked up her shoulder-bag and was standing, her head turned in search of Oncer. The conversation was nearly at an end and he saw her profile for the first time, beauty which missed being classical only through a lack of sentimentality which made her as modern as tomorrow.

'Quite a girl,' he said absently.

'She's simply...' Oncer hesitated. The words eluded him.

Mr Campion eyed the young man from above his spectacles. 'Would you tell her,' he said, 'that a man called Porteous, whom she knows, was somewhere near here last night and may still be hovering around. I'm afraid it won't be very long before he unearths your secret. He may look like something out of a horror comic but he isn't the ideal chap for fun and games, cops and robbers. I think he's about as safe to tangle with as a king cobra.

'If you're in touch with an elderly friend of hers tell him that he should send her back to Brett and keep right away from her until he's settled whatever his business is. Will you do that?'

Oncer avoided his eyes.

'I'll tell her what you said,' he mumbled. 'Though it won't be news to her. That fat

142

pig has been snouting around for quite a while, making trouble. A blasted nerve he's got. He dumped Anthea in her own car at the back of beyond because she caught him at it whilst he was searching Coastguards. If it hadn't been for someone who'd spotted the car being driven off from Brett that night – someone who was trying to contact her – she'd have been stranded. After that she sent for me, so I...'

He broke off, his colour deepening. 'I'm talking too much. Don't ask me what it's all in aid of because I simply don't know. I'm just a tame bodyguard as far as I can see.'

'She may need one. Remember the gipsy's warning and keep her away from Porteous and his chums.'

'I'm having a crack at it.' Oncer spoke without enthusiasm. 'You don't understand Anthea, though. I wish I did. Good-bye, sir. Nice to have seen you again.'

He edged through the crowd towards the girl as she approached and took her by the elbow, piloting her out of the room. In the alcove the man in the blue shirt had re-seated himself with his back to the company. He had opened a notebook and was studying it, his pencil hesitating above the page.

As the pair turned the corner into the main hall a man who had been standing at the bar nodded to the figure by the door who sidled away out of sight.

Before Mr Campion reached the hall three men were ahead of him, moving casually towards the entrance. The approach to the Drover's Arms was by way of a wide tarmac drive facing on to a semi-circular lawn protected by posts and rails, now solidly lined with cars. He heard an engine starting and caught a glimpse of a bright scarf as a little blue Renault flashed past the open doorway. His progress was impeded by a man who stumbled into his path, kicked his ankle and apologized without looking round. A second car, a Mercedes, glided into sight and paused almost imperceptibly to allow the three men to scramble inside and vanish. The operation, smooth as steel, had taken less than thirty seconds. Mr Campion followed.

His own car was parked some distance down the drive and he had difficulty in extracting it, for later arrivals had inserted themselves without regard for a man who might wish to get away in haste.

The single street of Great Burdon was cluttered with sightseers, window shoppers and slow-moving traffic. He negotiated the hazards with as much speed as he dared but he had reached open country before the needle touched sixty. By Burdon Stone, where the ground was high and the road wound in a long erratic curve, he halted the car and ranged over each visible stretch of road with his field glasses. A little blue car, no larger now than a miniature toy seen across a nursery, appeared briefly on the far side of the Penuries and vanished beyond a fold of the hills, with the Mercedes a quarter of a mile behind.

He was half-way into his seat when the flash of blue caught his eye again, moving like a minnow between the seaweed green of late summer trees. Miss Peregrine and her companion were doubling back on their tracks, using the side road to Burdon forest.

Logic suggested that it would be possible to cut across country and intercept the chase but Mr Campion, remembering the twists of Cotswold lanes, decided to take no chances. He sped on through the lazy mid-day villages, passed a great estate landscaped by Capability Brown himself and followed the dictated route, hoping that high ground would give him a second view of the quarry.

The opportunity came sooner than he had expected. The vale of Burdon, still mantled in part by the forest, slopes with surprising steepness at a point where the by-road which bisects it is comparatively straight. Below him, less than four hundred yards distant, the Mercedes was halted and a single figure stood beside it, his back turned.

Mr Campion ran his own car into the obscurity of the trees and made his way prudently through bracken and brambles until he had halved the distance. The reason for the halt became clearer.

Ahead of the Mercedes, just off the road on the far side, the little blue car lay at an ominous angle half engulfed in a ditch. Through his binoculars he could distinguish the features of a man who had evidently been searching the interior. He stumbled awkwardly on to the bank, looked about him as he brushed his kneecaps and gestured to the remaining figure, directing him into the woods.

The search seemed unlikely to succeed for the undergrowth offered cover which would have defied an army of beaters and within ten minutes one of the party re-appeared and opened the door of the Mercedes, sounding the horn several times. The summons took some time to be answered. It was repeated twice before the last of the quartet emerged far up the lane and strode back to the group.

A conference followed, assisted by lengthy reference to a map which was unfolded on the bonnet but it did not appear to conjure complete agreement. One of the party broke away to search the abandoned car for a second time, returning with a road book and another map. It was impossible for the watcher to decide whether the final additions had brought inspiration but the effect was a decision. The four men bundled into the Mercedes and drove off at speed.

Mr Campion extracted his personal

transport from its seclusion and approached the Renault without concealment. The offside wheels were deep in the ditch but no damage was apparent. He made no attempt to search the interior and since the ignition key was missing he could do nothing to discover if it was still roadworthy.

He returned to his own car and sounded the horn, higher in tone than the Mercedes, in a series of uneven toots, repeating the performance some seconds later and following it with a long burst which might possibly be construed as an 'all clear'. The call faded into silence, the birds returned to their normal twitter but there was no other response.

He had reversed his Jaguar with some difficulty and was on the point of returning to the Drover when a small breakdown van bearing the sign 'Beadles' Garage, Great Burdon', passed him and drew into the verge on tyres which complained peevishly at the affront. A young man, cheerful and tow-haired in brown dungarees, descended.

'It wasn't you that phoned?'

'Not guilty,' said Mr Campion. 'I only stopped to see if there was any trouble. How long since you had the message?'

'Ten minutes. We're not that quick as a rule but I happened to be going this way on another job. Nothing really wrong by the look of it – just a tow-in and wait till called for. Some people are round the bend. A kid of ten could winkle this out if he used his loaf.'

'It was a man who called you? Did he give a name?'

'He said Smith, which makes you think a bit. I wouldn't have come out if he hadn't offered proof. Half a mo.' He opened the nearside door of the Renault and fumbled for some time under the dashboard, twisting his body ridiculously in the process. Finally he emerged with an envelope which had evidently been stuck into the recess with gum tape. It contained a five pound note and a car key.

'He's the owner all right. Emergency ration in case he's caught short. He told me where to look. It's mostly women who go in for that trick. They do it with all sorts of things – hatpins, lipstick, love letters. You'd be surprised.'

'Some women,' said Mr Campion judicially, 'are remarkably bright in an emergency.'

12

Private Investigation

George Lampeter, who was standing in a doorway on the corner of Valet Street, Soho, where it joins Fitzroy Street, was enjoying his day's work in his own methodical fashion. It had started in Hendon just before eight in the morning and his business had taken him to Kensington, thence to Sotheby's auction rooms, to a group of stockbrokers' offices in the city, to an oriental carpet dealer's shop in Wigmore Street, and brought him at half-past five to a shabby row of houses whose grimy faces were still dignified by some of the finest Queen Anne porches in London. Number Seven, the entrance which was of particular interest to him, had an intricate semicircular fanlight surrounded by a classic overmantel. On the flat supporting columns a number of brass enamel plates displayed the names of the firms doing business within. Apart from 'S. Knopf, Tailor' none of them was informative but the watcher had quartered the area before and one of them at least was no longer a mystery.

W. Carpenter & Co. were almost exactly

what their name suggested. They occupied the rear of the ground floor and a considerable workshop at the back built on what once had been a strip of garden. Here they restored, reconstructed, changed and sometimes created antique furniture with the unhurried skill of dedicated craftsmen. A set of Sheraton chairs multiplied from six to a dozen, yet each of them still contained enough material for it to be certified as genuine. Apparently ruined pieces returned to their magnificent middle age, tables matured by a century in a matter of days and panelling became so decayed that to question its authenticity was ludicrous. The four old men and a boy who gave their time to Carpenter & Co. performed their timely miracles with placid impartiality. They were paid handsomely for their skills and discretion was as much a part of their characters as the pale flower in the centre of old oak.

Lampeter waited and watched whilst Morris Jay, who was a regular visitor, paid his call and departed. There was nothing more to be gathered from his movements, which repeated a pattern now becoming wearisome. It was not important to discover whether or not he owned the firm but it was probable that he was at least a partner.

The craftsmen left in a body, with Old Ted, the foreman who kept the firm's keys, bringing up the rear. The front door remained open for the benefit of other business interests until eight, when the resident caretaker, a metal engraver who lived and worked in the basement, locked up for the night. He was a silent man, a member of a religious body called the Heirs of Boaz whose secret tenets, whatever they were, did not include a belief in fresh air or cleanliness.

By ones and twos the workers appeared in the doorway, said their good nights and scattered on their lawful occasions. Lampeter recognized them all. Pettigrew, thin, threadbare and scholarly who dealt in rare butterflies, Mrs Isadore with her two daughters who re-modelled fur coats and Dr Chattergee who dispensed the Mystic Herbal Remedies of the East by mail order only.

Simpkin & Talbot (Workshops) remained. The firm occupied the floor over Carpenter's in the annexe, which was comparatively new, an uncompromising brick box built to comply with the minimum Government requirements laid down for working conditions. Only two men toiled for Simpkin & Talbot, brothers who were unmistakably twins, small grizzled men who came and went in unison and were so united in thought that they appeared to communicate without conversation.

Lampeter, a thorough man, had failed to discover their business or indeed anything about them except that their name was

Worth. Tonight, he decided, was the time to tidy that problem so that it could be eliminated from his list. It was the sort of detail which he enjoyed since the two men he had assigned to watch the activities of Morris Jay had not considered it merited attention.

He folded the newspaper which was providing him with an excuse for loitering in an opposite doorway and tucked it under his arm when they appeared, waddling purposefully, side by side and in step. Across Charlotte Street they turned into the jumble of passages and narrow ways which form the northern fringe of Soho. After the third turning Lampeter had decided where they were heading and he followed them into the aromatic twilight of Twiggs Wine Lodge with the confidence of an habitué.

The narrow L-shaped room with its tables made from sherry casks and sawdusted floor had not changed in his adult lifetime and he was reminded of his youth when white port had been considered an upper-class aperitif by those of student age. The barman too had not changed within living memory and he recalled his name – Nobby.

Good sherry at remarkably low prices was the speciality which drew and held the patrons of the house so that the majority of the customers were regulars known to one another at least by sight. The brothers were installed in a corner, sitting facing each other, two identical measures on the barrel between them, as he eased his way to the farther end of the small curved bar.

'Good evening, sir. Your usual?'

Lampeter appreciated a man who, like himself, could remember a face after a lapse of years.

'I'm drinking fino now, Mr Clarke. Times change. Too old for the sweet stuff.'

It was some time before he could pursue his business: drinking at Twiggs was understood as part of civilized living, not a matter to be hurried. Ten minutes went by, during which one of the twins had been making calculations which were evidently complicated on the back of a letter. He passed the result across the table to his brother who shook his head. An adjustment, carefully considered, followed and the sheet was re-presented. The man with his back to the company nodded, the document was pocketed, the glasses emptied and the pair withdrew in undisturbed unity.

'A rum couple,' said Lampeter casually. 'Like an old-time music hall act. D'you know them?'

The barman was proud of his omniscience and anxious to underline his welcome to the returning prodigal. Deliberately he broke one of the first rules of his profession.

'The Worth brothers,' he said. 'It's a matter of twenty years since they started coming here and I can just tell them apart. It's Mr Worth who buys the drinks. He has a signet ring on the little finger of the left hand. The other is the other Mr Worth – that's what they all call him.'

He put down the glass which he had been polishing. 'I'm not being funny, though I am, if you follow me. A gentleman came in here last week looking for one of them. "Has Mr Worth been in?" he said. "Which Mr Worth?" I said. "The other Mr Worth," he said. Then I knew who he was talking about.'

Lampeter was impressed.

'Extraordinary. I suppose they aren't really a cabaret act? What do they do for a living?'

The atmosphere at Twiggs Wine Lodge had much in common with a club. The barman threw the topic into open discussion.

'I've often wondered myself. Mr Phillips here might know – or Mr Bernard.'

'They make watches.'

'They repair delicate instruments – cameras, compasses, balances, microscopes – that sort of thing.'

'Scientific equipment.'

'Pocket computers.'

Into the welter of suggestion the man addressed as Phillips thrust a muscular wrist embellished with a black dial which might have been designed as part of the instrument panel of an airliner.

'Watches. I know it for a fact. I showed this

to the other Mr Worth last year after it had been losing a second a day on the alarm. He put it right by the next evening and wouldn't even take a drink. I'd had the best people in London on it and they were all beaten – couldn't touch the problem. They're very high-class watchmakers. Swiss, if you want to know.'

Having settled the discussion the authority retreated to his crossword puzzle. Lampeter emptied his glass and, since etiquette and goodwill demanded the gesture, called for another.

The difficulty he found in collecting his change from the bar at first puzzled and within seconds alarmed him. He bent down to retrieve an elusive florin which had found its way to the floor. The world swam. Two florins eddied over a carpet of sawdust amongst a forest of feet. His hat dropped from his head to join the confusion. Strong hands helped him to unfold.

'Steady, old man. Take it easy.'

'He needs a breath of air.'

'I'll see him home. I know where he lives. My car's just outside.'

The barman summed up the incident after it had been decorously concluded. 'You don't know who your friends are,' he said, 'until something goes wrong.'

13

The Lampeter Report

L.C. Corkran was extremely irritated by the memo which lay in front of him. Long experience of the Establishment had taught him a contempt for that body which he had not always bothered to conceal for there had been times when the effort was not, in his opinion, worth making. He was a fair-minded, if cynical man and when the blame for a mistake lay rightly or wrongly at his door he never attempted to pass it along the corridor. Above him had been career men whom he despised, politicians whom he regarded as obstacles to be overcome in the light of their individual ambitions or prejudices. Below him there had been trustworthy men of his own choice.

Now the situation was almost reversed. He had respect for the intelligence of the Boardroom if not for its integrity, for its members for the most part had come up the hard way and knew precisely what they were about even when they disagreed. Of his staff he was less certain, for they were his by inheritance.

Even the extra card he had introduced into the pack had not produced the trick. Campion in his opinion had certain merits but this time they had been eclipsed. Across the enormous desk – Omega did nothing on a small scale – he contemplated his old friend with disapproval, one eyebrow raised and the other contracted in a frown.

'Lampeter has put in a report,' he said, 'which is very disturbing. It does not confirm your information of last week and in fact it suggests that we have been misled – a calculated piece of deception which was very nearly successful. I take it you know of this development?'

'I know that the man who died at Great Burdon was not Makepeace,' said Mr Campion mildly. 'And that his name was not Matthews either. Has Lampeter discovered who he really was?'

'It seems highly probable.' Corkran was formal in his displeasure. 'I think you should read this.' He reversed the folder and skimmed it across the desk.

Re Francis Makepeace:

(1) Responsible witnesses at Great Burdon (Dr Hector Penn, Anthony Cyril Morgan, bank manager, and Alfred Dimsdale, wine waiter at the Drover's Arms) have confirmed that the photographs produced are not of the man known to them as Matthew James Matthews, deceased.

157

(2) The waiter Dimsdale and the head bar-man, Leonard Caldecott, both think the photo-graph produced is of a man who occasionally visited the hotel but neither is a reliable witness on this point. The Drover has a large tourist clientele and a smaller cadre of regular or local patrons. Makepeace was certainly not one of the latter category or he would be remembered.

(3) Thomas James McArdie, 64, ship's engin-eer of Elmdene, 47, Woodthorpe Road. Forest Hill, SE was employed by Omega (Marine Research Division – Western) from September 1927 to October 1939 and from April 1946 until retirement on full pension (£1,200 p.a.) four years ago, having served in the Merchant Navy in the interval, becoming Chief Engineer. Most recent photograph on file shows him as a man with receding hair, possibly prematurely aged. Medical check on retiring from Omega records cardiac murmur, not thought to be serious provided sufficient care was exercised.

He had been living at irregular intervals with his eldest daughter Mrs Elizabeth Morrow who owns the house where he has his own self-contained flat, in the upper part. I have exam-ined these rooms and found nothing relative to this inquiry. They contain a great quantity of technical equipment, tape recorders, cameras, short-wave transmitting sets, stereo record-players, etc. McArdie seems to have enjoyed collecting and bartering these objects as a hobby though he does not appear to have used them for the purpose for which they were designed. The daughter confirms this and states that the habit runs in the family. She also states that McArdie used or possessed a Rover motor-car No CXF 072 E which has a dealer's re-sale value of £1,200, somewhat beyond his income bracket, even assuming he had saved prudently.

(4) The car CXF 072 E is identified as registered to Matthew Matthews and was recovered by the police from the sea off Brett Ness, Suffolk, in the course of their inquiries into the death of Max Newgate, manager of the Drover's Arms.

(5) Thomas McArdie was known to Makepeace who was senior geologist whilst McArdie was serving in the company's research ships, the **Cappa Omega** and the **Delta Omega**, a period of seven years.

(6) McArdie has not been seen by his daughter since the alleged death of Matthews.

(7) It is confirmed by the Coroner's Officer (P.C. Leatherdale) at Great Burdon and by Dr Penn that the deceased wore an expensive wig which was not detected until after death. They describe a photograph of McArdie without wig as being 'very like' the man they knew as Matthews.

(8) A man named Matthew Matthews, who died in 1960, worked for Petroleum Bruxelloise and was known to be a friend of Makepeace's, who was an executor of the will. This would explain the existence of genuine identity papers, etc., which must have been used to establish

159

*Matthews as a bona fide person for tax pur-
poses, etc., in Great Burdon.*

I therefore conclude:

*(a) That the body buried at Great Burdon is
that of Thomas James McArdie and that he
died a natural though unexpected death from
heart trouble. There is now strong evidence of
collusion between him and Francis Makepeace
for a purpose yet to be ascertained.*

(b) Francis Makepeace is still alive.

I am continuing my efforts to trace him.

Mr Campion put down the folio.

'Very thorough,' he said. 'Lampeter's a
sound man and a quick worker. Respectfully,
I can only agree with every word he says. I
wish him fortune.'

Corkran cleared his throat. 'I gather you
made some helpful suggestions. Some of
them seem to have borne fruit. On the next
page of Lampeter's report there is a reference to the mysterious Mr Morris Jay who
appears to lead an energetic if blameless life.
He was seen in Great Burdon quite recently
but he has respectable reasons for being
here. Lampeter has increased our watch on
the man, but I am not optimistic about the
results. He may prove to be the proverbial
red herring. Do you concur?'

'Not altogether.' Mr Campion rejected the
temptation to compete with the resident
professional and added diffidently, 'I think

there could be another interest in Mr Jay's life. Certainly his official business is quite genuine – remarkably successful. His reputation in the trade is high. I have this fancy that he has two strings to his bow – nothing stronger.'

'If he has,' said Corkran dryly, 'Lampeter will dig it out. I've put his nose out of joint already by introducing a man he regards as a casual interloper into the brew so he's on his mettle. Leave Jay to him, and it may restore his self-respect. He needs some encouragement. Read the last page.'

The final folio consisted of a single paragraph.

Mr Albert Campion had some conversation with a person unknown to me near Burdon Stone on the 17th inst. As instructed I kept observation on this meeting but the conversation appeared to be friendly. No doubt you will be informed of what took place. Mr Campion told me that the subject's name was Claude Porteous. I saw but did not recognize the man and do not believe he is in any way connected with the oil industry. Inquiries to date from usual informants have produced no information.

The visitor looked over his glasses.
'Usual informants?'
'He means,' said Corkran, 'the Criminal Record Office. Don't forget he was a police-

man once and he still has a friend or two in the upper reaches. Very useful at times as you know from personal experience. Tell me about Porteous.'

Mr Campion obliged. His account, within limits, was colourful and accurate.

'You were right about the possibility of bribery,' he concluded. 'I was offered quite a handsome sum for any information I could contribute. Porteous, whoever he is or whatever he represents, is just as interested as we are and is spending a lot of money in the hope of keeping ahead of us. He's a noteworthy type – once seen never forgotten – so he must be on somebody's file. Could it be an old one of yours?'

He looked across the expanse of green leather towards Corkran who was grimacing to himself, thoughtfully but without amusement.

'The assumption is confirmed,' he said. 'My late Department has had its eye on Claude Huxtable Porteous for twenty years. Despite his bulk he remains a shadowy figure and that means that he keeps to the background in his deals, always using nominees or companies registered in Luxembourg or South America which are difficult to unearth. I suppose he could be called an international agent, which is meaningless as a phrase.'

He paused, his eyes half closed, his head

lifted. 'I must do better than that if I am to bandy classified information between one ex-colleague and another. Porteous has been suspected of dealing in top secrets – commercial espionage – on three occasions, but nothing was ever confirmed. He certainly has no loyalties in the political sense and is probably a high-powered catalyst, which makes him both dangerous and untrustworthy, since even the criterion of money does not always apply directly to his motives – it could be power he was after, a lever to enforce some movement in quite another sphere. A difficult man to put in a category. I recall a case in point ten years ago. The French were making enormous strides in hydro-electric power and anything they do is always subject to peripheral corruption – they understand the art of the *pourboire* better than any other nation except perhaps the Turks – and regard it as a normal part of commercial life. One particular deal interested us because it might have involved patents which were still on our secret list and it looked very much as if one of the contractors not only knew all about them but intended using them, which might have caused a lot of unpleasantness. Yet they never did – they withdrew their tenders and dropped right out of the running. That suited our book even if we couldn't claim the credit.

'Within one month they were in Queer

Street and their assets were sold to a minor rival. Porteous was around at the time but we could never pinpoint his connection, though it certainly existed.'

'Commercial blackmail?'

Corkran shrugged his shoulders.

'Pressure of some sort, undoubtedly. Blackmail is a useful portmanteau word and we thought it more likely than simple bribery. The big kill must have come much later on – perhaps two mergers away.

'Information appears to be his stock-in-trade. I cannot say that I enjoy the idea that he is trying to get hold of Makepeace.'

Mr Campion allowed himself time to digest the information.

'Anything on the personal side of the Porteous dossier?' he inquired. 'Habits, hobbies, tastes, state of health, last known address and so on?'

'Very little.' Corkran made the admission gloomily, casting his mind back to an unsatisfactory episode. 'Asthmatic, if I remember, fat, and addicted to tautology, but you have seen him. He looks like a screen villain and cultivates the air. Habits – greedy in a gourmet manner. I once saw him eating a meal at the Carlton in Cannes and it was a disgusting sight. He took about three mouthfuls – the best – out of each of half a dozen expensive dishes, and gave me the feeling that his main pleasure was the disapproval of the *maître*.

164

He may treat women in the same way but we've no real information, though Helen Diaz, an actress by designation and a courtesan by nature, once spent a week at a château near Grenoble in his company. We gathered that she did not enjoy the experience. No fixed address that we could trace, and that is typical. He may well own that château under a company name, or even some of the hotels he uses. I think it would be correct to say that obscurity is an obsession with him. The psychiatrists – whom I mistrust – would say it was a compensating reflex for his repulsive and noticeable appearance.

'And yet, you know, he cannot resist a touch of theatre. He enjoys making his opponents appear ridiculous. After all our investigations into the hydro-electric business, which we hoped had been carried out completely under cover, he sent me a box of cigars, my own Romeo y Juliettas, with his card enclosed. They were very nearly taken away for analysis but we established that the order had been posted direct from Lambert's in Duke Street and that Porteous had never been near the place. It was a gesture of contempt, but I let it go up in smoke.'

'And now,' said Campion, 'he finds time to wander round England in a pantechnicon, which I think is an effective disguise for a caravan, looking for Makepeace.'

Corkran scowled. He was a handsome man but the contortion made his face a shade short of comic. He took a deep breath, exhaled it slowly, and spoke with unusual vehemence.

'I want him off my territory,' he said. 'I will not have that pot-bellied schemer interfering in my affairs. Before, we had only an indirect interest in his behaviour but now he could cause real damage. What are the chances of getting a criminal charge brought against him?'

'Over the death of Newgate, the hotel man?'

'You suggested there might be a connection. Could it be strengthened – ponderously investigated – with some discreet string pulling from above? Enough pressure to frighten him off?'

Mr Campion considered the proposition.

'It's possible, but unlikely, I'd say. Either he had nothing to do with it or the thing was done by employees who got panicky. In any case he would be well protected. You'll probably find that he can prove he wasn't even in the country.'

Corkran subsided. He was aware that his outburst had been over-emphasized and he allowed himself time to cool.

'Softly, softly, then,' he said. 'If he's put under constant surveillance – and is aware of it – then his position may become untenable. He will be forced to delegate authority to men who may be more open to attack.'

'First catch your hare,' murmured Mr Campion. 'He may not be easy to locate. He...'

A subdued buzz from one of the telephones on the desk interrupted him. Corkran lifted the receiver.

'Yes?' he said and listened for some time. 'I see ... and this was last night? You've spoken to him ... seen him? Good. I don't think you need worry about the Press but put it in Mitchell's hands straight away. He saw to that himself? Very sensible.' Again he listened as a muffled gibber came over the wire. 'I see. A very unlikely story so it may be true. By the way, I suppose there is no previous history of this sort of thing? Good. Thank you for telling me.' He rang off, his face dark with irritation.

'That was Mrs Devenish, my invaluable mentor. It seems that Lampeter was arrested last night in Leicester Square just after closing time, found in the gutter drunk and incapable. He was fined five pounds at Bow Street this morning and the Magistrate singled him out for a homily on his behaviour. Thank God we're big enough to kill the story.

'His own account of his adventures is so melodramatic that no one would give it credence. Kidnappers, drugged drinks and so on...What he was pleased to call a Mickey Finn. At least he had the good sense to plead guilty.'

Mr Campion sighed.

'It has the Porteous touch,' he said.

14

The Pigeon-hole

The telephone was ringing with the weary persistence which that instrument seems to acquire when the summons has been long unanswered. Mr Campion, who had just unlocked the door of his London flat, dived towards it with the conviction that he was going to be too late and was proved right by a hand's breadth.

It remained silent until late in the afternoon, a smug reproach for neglect and a proof of the characteristic which it holds in common with watched pots. On the second occasion, however, he caught the connection before the bell could throb twice. The voice was soft but so deep that although the tone was no louder than a whisper it was clear and individual.

'Mr Campion? You do not know me, so I must introduce myself. My name is Morris Jay.'

'Of Knightsbridge? Walnut and Dutch marquetry?'

'That is my special province. You and I appear to have other interests in common. I wonder if you would consider discussing them? Without prejudice, as the lawyers say.'

'I have an affection for marquetry.' Campion's murmur was equally bland. 'Shall I drift along for a chat – or would you like to come here?'

The unquestioning acceptance seemed to surprise the caller. There was a pause before the velvet voice replied.

'Would you bear with me if I proposed a compromise? I have a great dislike for people who pry into my affairs and recently nearly every move I make has been spied upon, sometimes by a man called Lampeter whom I've seen in your company, sometimes by people I think may be connected with him, and now there appear to be new observers. At first it was amusing but the performance has become wearisome. I would like to be private.'

'What do you suggest?'

'A little stratagem. There is a basement restaurant in Bond Street, almost opposite the auction rooms called The Pigeon-hole. It is a meeting-place for members of my trade and we have our own room there – not a club, you understand, but a place reserved for our use. There is a back entrance in Maddox Arcade, number 12, for the use of the staff and the tradesmen. If you go down the staircase the second door on your right opens directly into our room, where we can be quite alone. Could you be there in, say, an hour?'

'No password?'

The ghost of a laugh flickered on the line.

'I shall be there to greet you. My own humour will be to evade my shadows now that I have learned their habits. In my case there is nothing to excite them about my visit since the place is within my normal orbit, but I intend to arrive without an escort.'

'In an hour, then.'

'There is just one other point. It occurs to me that you, too, may be under observation. By all means take precautions if you feel you are being led into some sort of trap – I can imagine how this conversation could be construed – but it might be less embarrassing for both of us if our meeting went unrecorded.'

'I'll do my best,' said Mr Campion. 'No elaborate disguise – just simple evasive action.'

It was half-past six, the hour when the tide of business has ebbed from Mayfair and senior executives consider it respectable to take the first official drink of the evening. At a corner in Bruton Street where The Two Linkmen offers refreshments and quilted upholstery in equally expensive proportions, Mr Campion entered by one of three curtained doors and escaped immediately through another, moving by a series of cuts to the near end of Maddox Arcade. His shadow, if he existed, had been defeated by the manoeuvre and he slipped into the opening marked 12 unobserved. The nostalgic scent of France marched to greet him as he descended the wooden stairs, a mixture of scrubbing soap, caporal, and garlic which rarely survives the cross-channel journey. The handle of the second door on the right refused to answer and he tapped lightly. A narrow crack appeared through which a single eye inspected him with suspicion.

'You wish Mr Jay?'

'I think he's expecting me.'

From behind the figure a deeper voice gave an instruction.

'Let him in, Nicko. Lock it again and leave us alone. I'm perfectly all right now – nothing to worry about. If I need anything I'll ring.'

Mr Campion found himself in a small room which might have come straight from provincial France. It was heavy with Breton oak and decorated with copper pans. Morris Jay sat at the table in the centre, his head bowed and his hands clasped round a wine glass. One shoulder was wet with mud and, when he looked up, the dark smear continued across the side of his face and bedraggled the receding curls about his forehead, giving him the melancholy expression of a sheep who has escaped from a storm.

His blue shirt had been pulled open at the neck.

'Forgive my appearance. I had some difficulty on the way.' He rubbed his cheek and examined the mud on a hand which was grazed and crusted with blood. The suggestion of affectation in the voice was emphasized by the effort to speak coherently. 'I suppose that I am in a state of shock. There is refreshment in the armoire, so please make yourself comfortable. Perhaps you could bring me some Calvados.'

'You had an accident?'

The man in the chair was trying to breathe normally but the effort was painful.

'I asked for trouble, one supposes. I attempted to evade my watchdogs by changing tube-trains at the last moment – I spoke to you from Hendon, where I live – and the strategy excited them. At Marble Arch, when I thought I had been successful, there was a scuffle on the pavement as I tried to get into a taxi. An effort perhaps to frustrate me or castigate my impertinence. I offered no resistance ... just tried to escape ... the passing crowd came to my rescue.' He swayed his head experimentally and winced. 'That is really all I can say. I am bruised but not injured.'

Mr Campion poured Calvados from a hand-labelled bottle and found himself a whisky and soda.

'Something of the sort happened once before. Any connection, or just the natural hazards of the trade?'

Jay's dark eyes, one of which was becoming puffy, opened wide.

'You know of that incident?'

'Just what was in the papers.'

'There is no connection, or very little. I was attacked that night, not for money, but for what might be called information. I was searched but not robbed.'

He took a mouthful of spirit and mopped his face ruefully with a bandanna silk handkerchief.

'I thought we should meet because your face is new to me in this business. I don't go out of my way to make enemies of business rivals — they are better as acquaintances, even friends. You are associated with this man Lampeter who is behaving like a policeman yet is not a policeman and so must have a commercial employer. You are evidently in a superior position, nearer to the fountainhead. You seemed approachable, civilized. Could you declare your interests?'

Mr Campion did not reply immediately. He offered a spotless handkerchief in replacement for the sodden bundle in Jay's hand and sipped his whisky.

'My problem is the late Matthew Matthews,' he said, 'or rather his partner with whom I think you're in contact. Several people want to talk to him urgently and you seem to be ahead of the queue. It's as simple as that.'

Jay was dissatisfied. He massaged his neck and hesitated, putting his thoughts in order.

'Unless you can be a little more specific we may both be wasting our time. There is a man called Porteous who is also spending time and money on this chase. I cannot be certain but I believe that it was his people who tried to get hold of me this evening: this attack was probably a warning not to be too clever. Until very recently, a month ago, I had never heard of him, so he is not, so to speak, a member of the club. You may not wish to answer the question, but are you connected with him?'

'I've met him.' Mr Campion was cautious. 'But we have nothing in common except curiosity.'

Jay did not respond. The meeting had not gone as he had expected, he was frowning and the contraction of his injured forehead was painful.

'I wonder,' said Mr Campion at last, 'if we are at cross-purposes. Mr Jay, apart from antiques, what are your interests? You said we had something in common. I need to find this missing partner for excellent reasons connected with his past career but I suspect that you have something quite different in mind. Could you lift that curtain?'

175

The question deepened the change of temperature. Jay closed his eyes as if he were aware that his mind had been dulled by physical shock and was fighting himself to keep control of the meeting. Slowly he assimilated an idea which brought surprise and suspicion in its wake. Before he answered he emptied his glass.

'You are quite sure of what you are implying? Or are you being unnecessarily naïve?'

'I'm curious about your second interest – the one you thought we might have in common.'

The victim turned his head slowly.

'You assure me of that? You have no idea, even after all this prying into my affairs?'

'I was hoping to find out,' said Mr Campion mildly. 'After all that is why I came here.'

Jay was amused. He poured more Calvados and stretched his back: his strength was returning.

'In that case,' he said, 'I can only apologize for making an elementary mistake. If you don't know, then I have no intention of telling you. There are too many greedy fingers reaching out already and it would be lunacy to add to them. Please forgive me – I have no intention of being offensive. If your business and mine do not coincide then I can neither help nor hinder you. I apologize most sincerely for my stupidity.' He half turned his back, withdrawing his personality into a privacy which was inviolable.

Mr Campion accepted defeat.

'If your adventure tonight is a sample,' he suggested mildly, 'then you will have to be very careful when you next contact Miss Anthea Peregrine. You could be running her into a lot of trouble. Telephone her, write to her if you must, but don't meet her.'

Jay shrugged his shoulders, blinking at the twinge of pain which followed.

'She was a messenger, no more. In any case that young woman is very capable of looking after herself. Of course, you are right, but you must agree that I am not responsible for her. I must mind my own business, which you have just assured me is nothing to do with you. Perhaps we should change the subject. If you are interested in walnut you should visit my gallery, Mr Campion.'

'But I have. There is a baroque chest on a stand in the window. William and Mary?'

'Of that period. Not Dutch, as it appears, but Italian, though I bought it in Holland. Veneered seaweed marquetry about 1699 – quite perfect – the most beautiful piece I have had through my hands in thirty years.'

On the first of his particular subjects Morris Jay became a different man. Before Mr Campion could escape he had made an expensive purchase which instinct told him could not be the once-in-a-lifetime bargain it appeared.

Among Mr Jay's several accomplishments salesmanship had a dominating position.

15

The Messenger

Saffrons' Bank disputes with one other illustrious name the claim to have honoured the first cheque ever drawn in the city of London. *'Pray pay my good friend, Jno. Buck twenty of the new guineas.'* The instruction in the Duke of Lansdowne's cavalier copperplate still hangs in the Directors' room, the porter wears a green uniform with brass buttons and a cockaded top hat and the clerks appear to the customers in formal black even if their trousers reveal more modern taste. The head office in Pall Mall is carpeted so that only the rustle of notes and the humble chink of a coin disturbs an atmosphere ponderous with the scent of ink and paper-clips.

The appearance of a girl wearing a white crash helmet and jeans attended dutifully by a young man dressed almost identically raised several eyebrows, for Saffrons discouraged any outward display of modernity.

'My name is Peregrine,' she announced. 'The manager is expecting me and I am to give him a letter personally.' She took off her headgear and handed it to her escort, releasing a halo of bronze curls.

The clerk, whose delaying phrase was halfway to his lips, swallowed the words. She was not at all what he had been expecting, and he became avuncular. 'Of course, madam, this way.'

She consigned her companion to a leather settee and disappeared into a Georgian writing-room, apparently unaware of a minor triumph: even senior executives expected a decent interval at Saffrons before being received into hallowed privacy.

Mr Saffron Armitage, a cadet branch of the original family, emerged through an inner door after the briefest of delays, bearing a black metal deed box which he placed reverently on the baize surface of what had once been a Regency gaming table. He was a willowy young man who contrived deliberately to suggest diplomacy rather than banking. If the appearance of his visitor surprised him he concealed the fact. He read the letter which she presented and broke into a smile: either the contents or the style amused him. 'Shall I unlock this for you?'

She opened the leather satchel which had been hanging from her shoulder, produced a small purse and passed a key across the table, 'Please. And I should like some paper. Mr Makepeace told you, I expect, that I would be making some notes.'

'Mr Makepeace said that you knew exactly

what he wished and that we were to give you every assistance. It is some time since I saw him though he rang me up yesterday. I hope he's well?'

'Very fit indeed,' said Miss Peregrine formally. The deed box contained a quantity of documents, a batch of letters tied with fading blue ribbon, a silver christening mug, two daguerreotypes in leather cases, a gold locket with a miniature of a Victorian maiden on one side and a lock of hair on the other and a cheap office cash-box. She lifted each on to the table and began to sort them into related heaps.

'I may be some time,' she announced. 'When I've finished shall I ring a bell or just knock on your door?'

The last of the Saffrons hesitated. Rumours had been drifting into the rarefied air in which he moved and he was curious, but his client's instructions had been quite specific.

'Mr Makepeace isn't in town just now?' he ventured.

The girl looked up from the papers as if she had forgotten his existence.

'No,' she said. 'I expect he'll give you his new address when it's fixed.'

'There is some correspondence waiting for him. Perhaps you will tell him that?'

'Certainly.'

She bowed her head over the documents. Mr Saffron Armitage was forced to concede total defeat but he withdrew in good order.

In the outer hall of the temple the counter clerk slipped from his stool and drifted unobtrusively to the staff room, where for the convenience of the colleagues a private telephone box had been installed. He was away for some time: there were several profitable calls to be made.

Half an hour later Miss Peregrine emerged to rejoin her companion. She retrieved her helmet and checked her watch against the authority of the magisterial pendulum clock on the wall beside her.

'Just on twelve, Oncer. Let's get out of here and head into the country – a pub and something to eat. We've got all day so it doesn't matter where we go.'

The young man grinned. 'And half the night. Not before one, we decided, remember? You'll get fed up with riding pillion.'

'I am already. This tin hat weighs a ton. I can't wait to get back to a decent seat on four wheels. I've a damn good mind to risk it and just collect my car in the ordinary way.'

'You won't, you know. Today you're my responsibility.'

For the first time she treated him as her equal and the smile which acknowledged the intimacy of fellow conspirators made him feel like a giant. They recovered a motorcycle from its resting-place and bestrode the heavy machine professionally.

'Out towards Henley and Oxford,' he shouted above the roar of the engine. 'Leave it to me.'

For Oncer the day had the idyllic quality of a fairy-tale. He escaped knowledgeably from the city, took the arterial road to the west at a satisfying speed, abandoned it for by-ways at the right moment and discovered an inn which had not made any effort to attract long-distance attention. The afternoon died gloriously in a spectacular sunset and in the warm dusk a harvest moon hung like a Chinese lantern over Burdon woods. Beside the Stone they ate the last of their sandwiches and shared the final dregs of vacuum coffee. Oncer begrudged every passing moment. They were sitting formally like strangers newly introduced, on an oaken bench provided for visitors, the flask and the leather satchel between them, silent and deeply contented. Far behind them an occasional headlight marked the presence of the road to the Penuries, emphasizing the secret world which they alone shared.

Oncer stood up, stretching long arms into the sky.

'When did you first know,' he said. 'About old Matty, I mean – that he wasn't dead? Didn't it rock you a bit?'

She leaned forward, her elbows on her knees, her hands cupping her chin.

'Not a shock,' she said at last. 'Too slow

for that. I had a feeling it was part of a pattern which had gone wrong somewhere – as it had, of course. First it was the wrist-watch which I'd never seen him wearing. It was a very expensive job and not brand new. And some of the clothes which were left at the hotel didn't seem to belong. Then there was a pair of reading-glasses, very strong, which he never used when I saw him. But the car left in the garage – that cracking good Rover was certainly his. And the brief-case – the one with the trick bottom – was his. He always brought it down to Brett with him and I'd seen it plenty of times. It had nearly all his money in it, too.'

She paused and looked up, her smile clear in the moonlight. 'He has a wonderful nerve, the old pirate. Fantastic. He sneaked into the Drover where he and his chum had been going to meet and change places, so to speak, as soon as he knew I'd been given the case at the police station. I very nearly walked into him – and that would have been a shock – but he just burgled my room and got away with it. After all, it was his own money. If it hadn't been for that fat pig Porteous I'd never have known it existed. He was so damned inquisi-tive and mysterious that I wouldn't give him the satisfaction of looking as if I hadn't a clue what it was all about. He also said that Matty wore a wig, which I knew was nonsense.

'When Matty did turn up that morning in

184

the middle of nowhere I was so relieved to see a human face that I almost forgot he was supposed to be dead. Somehow I'd never quite believed the news in the first place. It seemed so – so unlikely that he would just die without warning.'

'I don't really see,' said Oncer doggedly, 'what those two old plotters thought they were up to – playing Box and Cox like that, I mean. Do you, honestly?'

'Discouraging nosy parkers. Anybody wanting to spy on Matthews at Great Burdon would discover that his forwarding address was at Brett. If they got as far as Brett they'd have found an entirely different Matthews, so they were back to square one. And vice versa, of course.'

'It's as clear as mud to me. Anthea, do you really know what it's all about? There's old Matty, as gay as a bee, older than God and having a ball as if he was some bloody young teenager. He's even had a haircut. Sometimes he makes me feel as if I was twenty-five or thirty. What the hell is he up to?'

Miss Peregrine gave the question the consideration it deserved.

'He's out to make a lot of money,' she said at last. 'Or he thinks he is. Fat Porteous thinks so too or he wouldn't be snooping around with his bunch of strong-arm men. Matty says that as long as I don't know anything I can't get into trouble and I can be useful to him. I had to talk him into that idea, so don't nark it.' She stood up. 'I think the old boy is having a new adventure when he'd begun to think he was past it. That's what keeps him young. I wish him luck.'

'Is that all? No guesses – no theories?'

'It suits me. You couldn't call life at Brett one long round of wild excitement. I don't want to spend my time marching around the place, shouting slogans and protesting – I'd rather do something with a real kick in it – wouldn't you?'

'You could bet on it.'

'Let's keep it mysterious then. The truth might be something ghastly like the plans for an oil refinery in Nicaragua or a merger in concrete on the Stock Exchange. Agreed?'

'Agreed.'

He picked up the satchel, slung it over his shoulder and held out his hand.

'There's hours yet. Let's spy out the countryside.'

The long trek through Burdon woods brought them at midnight to a road which was unexpected. They trudged for half a mile before a signpost confirmed that they had missed the track leading back to the Stone and were close to the T-junction where the Drover's Arms stood as outpost above the town. A narrow street of Tudor cottages carefully restored, each elegant as a collector's dolls' house, brought them to the side of

Beadles' Garage, closed and like the rest of the silent buildings apparently deserted. The breakdown van and a number of cars were ranged by the wall of an open concrete yard, among them the blue Renault, its colour deepened by moonlight.

'There she is,' said Oncer. 'Simple as falling off a log. You can drop me off to pick up the bike as we go back.'

Anthea put out a restraining hand. 'Keep still for a bit and make sure we're alone. There's somebody in that car parked across the High Street.'

Oncer strained his eyes, his head on one side.

'Courting couple, I think. Do we make a rush for it, or simply stroll in casually?'

'It's my own car. The bill's paid and I'm simply driving it off. We act accordingly.'

She led the way, stepping briskly from the pool of shadow in which they had been standing. The Renault started without protest and crawled cautiously into the side road. The narrow byway meandered in a gentle arc to the main Oxford road where a sharp left-hand bend brought them once more again to the Drover's corner.

By the time they had come full circle and were passing the front of Beadles' Garage the car which had been standing opposite had vanished. Oncer looked over his shoulder.

'We have a follower. D'you think you can

shake him off or dodge him? Try a burst of speed and nip off into the lanes. Forget about the bike.'

Anthea bent forward, her eyes concentrated on the long beam of the headlights. They were clear of the town, the little car surging forward very close to its utmost.

'This is where we came in,' she said. 'I'm not making any more cross-country runs at this hour. I've got an idea.'

'I hope it's a good one – they're still with us.'

'It's straight common sense, so don't fuss. They are following us because they think we will lead them direct to Matty, right? I said I'd see him by tomorrow morning and I'm damn well going to whatever happens. At the first turn when we're out of sight for a moment I'm going to nip out and into the nearest ditch. You take over and drive straight ahead – not to Matty, but back to Brett. That tells them nothing. I'll pick up the bike. Take the keys out of the locker and you can doss at the house for the rest of the night. Ring me in the morning. Have you got that?'

'I don't like it. That damn thing's too heavy for you.'

'Don't argue with me, young Smith. Do as I say – now.'

She pulled the car sharply in to the off-side, opened the door and leaned over the seat to snatch up her helmet and satchel. As

188

she turned back Oncer planted his lips over hers in a brief but determined kiss.

'I'm not arguing, Miss Anthea,' he said. Before he reached the driving-seat she had vanished.

16

Potter's Field

Mrs Devenish came into L.C. Corkran's office with the air of a housekeeper who had just put down her knitting and nipped in to make sure that the drawing-room fire was still burning nicely. She settled herself, plump and comfortable, at the corner of the desk to his left and exchanged one pair of glasses for another which she stowed carefully into a large and ferociously luxurious handbag.

Across the expanse of chromium and green leather she faced George Lampeter, upright and business-like, two folders open in front of him. Mr Campion alone appeared informal; the remaining chair in the office was designed to make any suggestion of alertness impossible.

'Are we all met?' he inquired.

Corkran ignored the inference.

'The object of this exercise,' he said, 'is co-ordination. Mrs Devenish has something of significance to tell us and I gather that Lampeter has a development to report. Mr Campion has made a contact which may or may not be important but the question will have to be considered. If some specific action has to be taken we should all know what is intended.' He paused to rub the stubble of his moustache with the knuckle of his forefinger.

'Mrs Devenish?'

She straightened her back and smiled at each of them in turn.

'I was dining last night with Miriam Steinbeck, the head buyer of Findlays,' she announced. 'At Guido's, on the balcony. I find it interesting because one can see all the other tables.'

Mr Campion had an instant picture of her which was new and totally unexpected. She was not, as he had supposed, a motherly secretary blessed with a long memory and simple loyalty but an astute business woman of a very definite type, one who enjoyed the good things of life in the company of her peers, women who were patrons of the better restaurants of the world, eating and doing business, gossiping. Guido's was the first choice of golden-pocketed gourmets and Findlay's dressed the wealthiest matrons in Southern England. Her own shapeless sensible two-piece probably came from there but the choice was unhappy. Had she been in any other enterprise she would have been a director, a status enjoyed by most of her friends. He eyed her over his glasses with a new respect.

'In the alcove, at the table Guido calls the Royal Box, there was a man who from his description could only be Mr Porteous. He was dining with Ewan Harcourt.'

She turned to Campion.

'In case you don't know him I'd better explain. Harcourt – Professor Harcourt, he is now – was Francis Makepeace's opposite number in Pan-World Oils for many years. We tried on two occasions to persuade him away from them and failed, which we found humiliating at the time. He discovered, or rather pioneered, the Southern Gulf field and he now lectures in Geology at Cambridge and sometimes of course on television. If he can afford to do that he must be extremely wealthy. He is half American, has an American wife and three children, one of whom is a brilliant painter. He's sixty-two, rather dashing in appearance – theatrical, but genuinely clever – and he still keeps a connection with Pan-W.'

Corkran allowed her information time for digestion.

'There are two inferences to be drawn from this,' he said. 'Both are unfortunate. The first is that this Makepeace business is no longer a mystery to Porteous. He has established, as we did, that Makepeace and Matthews are the same person. The whole wretched trick is exposed.' He raised an eyebrow towards Lampeter. 'You can explain this, I think?'

'I can. He used our methods and got the same results. I'm afraid Mr Campion and I were seen together at the Drover and my connection with Omega was established – nothing difficult about that since I registered there in my own name. Once or twice lately I have been tailed and I've spotted it. This means, as you all know, that there have been other occasions when the job has been more expertly done.

'Mrs Morrow, McArdie's daughter, is a talkative woman and she's in some distress about her father's disappearance. Not affection – it's the money that interests her. After I called there she had another visitor – she reported this to me – and she may have mentioned the name Makepeace along with her father's connection with Omega. No way of stopping her, that I could see. It would be dead easy to put two and two together.'

'Highly probable,' said Corkran gloomily. 'The second inference is even less acceptable and I cannot see that discussing it will help. You have something to add, Lampeter?'

The stocky man glanced at one of his folios, closed it and spoke in witness-box style. 'I have. Since the McArdie connection with this affair has been investigated I've had inquiries made about one or two other known associates of Mr Makepeace in his Company days. Only one of them proved significant – Captain Joseph Wilberforce who was master of the *Delta Omega* until he retired last year. He's been a very good company servant, a bit of a martinet I'd say. He lives at Godalming with his father who's ninety and his brother and family, two boys in the Merchant Navy. A well-run household, very ship-shape. The garden looks like a quarter-deck tarted up to receive a visiting admiral and a squadron of Wrens.

'Two days ago they had a visit from a man called Collins, a slick salesman type of operator with a long story about being a journalist on a geographical magazine, who asked a lot of questions and I gather was sent off with a flea in his ear. He got nothing out of the Captain except instructions to walk the plank. But the questions were interesting and Collins was so smooth that it was some time before he was suspected. Wilberforce rang me up, very hot under the collar, breathing fire and brimstone.'

He hesitated, a frown gathering on his square obstinate forehead. 'He mentioned a phrase which I didn't understand and he spoke as if I ought to. The Grand Serendi.'

Mrs Devenish flicked a query towards Corkran with her eyes and waited for his response. Lampeter had touched a raw spot and was immediately aware of the effect he had conjured. He stiffened defensively.

'It seemed important to mention it.'

Corkran pulled his chin into his collar

surveying the conference under twisted eyebrows. 'The Grand Serendi Archipelago,' he said primly. 'Indian Ocean.'

'Potter's Field.' Mrs Devenish produced the words as if they were sufficient explanations now that the cat was inescapably free of the bag.

'It means nothing to me.' Lampeter was openly irritated. 'Is this some skeleton in the family cupboard which is never mentioned, or straight company business that I ought to know about if I'm to be allowed to get on with the job? You can't have it both ways.' He placed one folio on top of the other and folded his arms, waiting. Corkran looked down his nose.

'Mrs Devenish, you were here at the time. The reports appear to have been edited by Big Brother – there is very little about it in the Makepeace file for example, except his technical findings which don't refer, *per se,* to the unfortunate side of the story. Perhaps you can give us all an outline.'

She turned her head uneasily. 'Mr Campion is not a member of the staff.'

'He is a technical adviser, if you want an official phrase,' said Corkran. 'A précis will be quite sufficient.'

'Very well then.' Mrs Devenish spoke like a good cook who is reluctant to part with a private recipe. 'Potter's Field, which is the name we gave to the area because it was originally discovered by Sir Charles Potter, one of our pioneers in research, was a complete and expensive failure – the worst, in fact, in the company's history.

'Serendi is one of the new independent African States. It used to he called the Bwanaland Protectorate, and it's not even in the Commonwealth any longer. The islands off the coast which go with it have always been called the Grand Serendi, and now they seem to be breaking up – minor revolutions in the usual communist style with the usual jargon but basically it means just straight local dictatorship on tribal lines. It's all too small and remote to make news because Serendi has no commercial importance to anyone, except collectors of tropical fish. A coelacanth was found there two years ago.

'Sir Charles always said there was a big potential in the area and produced some evidence but we never did much about it because of the difficulties of drilling and transport. In '61 we were looking for new development areas and we sent our research ship, the *Delta Omega,* out with a number one team under Francis Makepeace. It was there that he first met Mr McArdie.

'It was disastrous from the start. The equipment was damaged by a tornado and took time to replace. Then there were local problems, squabbles about rights – our agreements were hopelessly out of date and invalid, so we faced claims which were pure blackmail – one expensive delay after another. The conditions were appalling because of the heat and the boredom – nobody was allowed ashore – and in fact there was a mutiny. Two men were killed, another permanently crippled and we had the greatest difficulty in suppressing the whole story. A fever epidemic didn't help; it delayed our work by several weeks.

'In the end the project was abandoned, partly for political reasons but largely because of Mr Makepeace's report. He said the stuff there was not worth working. Apparently there had been volcanic changes and what Sir Charles had found was a small pocket on the mainland which would never pay a dividend.'

Corkran permitted himself a twisted smile.

'What he said in fact was "Serendi is a pimple on the backside of Africa and there is nothing to be squeezed out of it except poison". I am paraphrasing his rather more picturesque phrase, but that was the message. It seems to have been an effective piece of *obiter dictum* as far as the Board was concerned. We abandoned our research there, though we kept our nominal right to exploit the field – for what it was worth. Allowing for successive governments since then that means very little.'

'Professor Harcourt,' said Mrs Devenish,

making it clear that she had been interrupted, 'didn't agree. It was none of his business and we never knew for certain if he had anything more than theoretical knowledge. But in his lectures this year he described Serendi as the last great potential field to be left unexploited. No doubt he's pointed that out to Pan-World.

'Now he is dining with Mr Porteous. And Porteous has been spending a lot of time and money trying to get hold of Francis Makepeace. I don't pretend to understand the ramifications but the inference is quite clear.'

Mr Campion intervened, mild and apparently myopic.

'I know a little about Harcourt,' he said. 'He has a reputation for going anywhere for the sake of a good dinner or a little publicity. I think we should remember that Porteous has only just established the Makepeace–Matthews identity. Before, it was simply Matthews he was after. Now that he knows who the man is, he is moving very sharply – investigating his associates and trying to find out all he can about him. I don't think Porteous is interested in oil.'

He turned to Mrs Devenish. 'These two men who were killed in the mutiny – what actually happened?'

'A row arising out of grievances caused by sheer boredom. Conditions on the *Delta Omega* were bad and the men thought they

198

ought to have been allowed ashore, despite the fact that the ship had been forbidden to dock. It was anchored off Bundi, the main island, outside the limit. Six of the crew were down with fever and two others – natives of some sort – stole a boat and deserted.

'Several of the rest were caught trying to do the same thing and there was a fight. They had broken into the liquor store and they were armed. Two of them were knocked or thrown overboard and drowned – a thing which wouldn't have happened if they'd been sober, I imagine. A third man broke his pelvis. It was a most unsavoury episode. Captain Wilberforce behaved with tremendous courage, despite the fact that he was wounded in the thigh by a bullet. He and McArdie saved the situation.'

'And Francis Makepeace?'

'He wasn't even there. He had been flown out and was waiting to join the ship at Port Bundi. He didn't go abroad until the whole thing had been ironed out and we'd re-established our right to make experimental drillings.'

Corkran tapped his desk with a long finger.

'Irrelevant in my view. This whole business could be cleared up by ten minutes' conversation with Makepeace if we could find him. It may be nothing whatever to do with Omega, though to assume that would be quite wrong at this stage. The question is elementary – what are we doing to locate the man, Lampeter?'

'Everything possible.' He re-opened one of his folios. 'Yesterday morning Makepeace sent a messenger to his bank, a young woman called Peregrine and her boy-friend – both known to Mr Campion. What precisely she did there we don't know but she spent half an hour looking through his papers. Where they went after that we don't know because I wasn't tipped off about it until after they'd gone. But we do know one thing. Makepeace is still around and anxious not to show his face. The girl's home at Brett is under observation and sooner or later she or the boy will give us a lead. She's telephoned the house several times.

'Mr Campion had an interview two days ago with this Morris Jay, who's one of the likely contacts and no doubt he will tell us what happened when he has time to get around to it.'

He looked up. 'Incidentally Jay is, or was, being watched by people other than ourselves, presumably on instructions from Porteous. Our chaps, also keeping an eye on him, got him out of a spot of trouble when he was trying to get dodgy. It didn't lead anywhere – just back to Mr Campion.'

Corkran raised an eyebrow.

'Albert?'

'I got nothing helpful – just a piece of

marquetry which may or may not be a bargain.' He described the meeting in some detail, and turned to Lampeter with the deference due to authority. 'With one exception I'd say he was our best bet. He is almost certainly in touch with Makepeace, though I doubt if he knows where he is. Are we still keeping our eyes open in that direction?'

'All round the clock. We've got competition now, but it may pay off in the end – provided that I'm not hampered by lack of liaison.'

Lampeter was truculent. 'What's your one exception?'

Mr Campion uncrossed his long legs, stood up and settled himself on the arm of his chair.

'Porteous,' he said mildly, 'is a business man. That is, he's not a professional criminal in the ordinary sense of the word – like a safe-breaker, for example. But he is up to some pretty sharp practice and he's not really an active type physically. That means he is being forced into using small-time crooks and strong-arm men recruited as best he can, a fact he doesn't bother to conceal. It suggests, don't you think, that he is using an agent as a recruiting officer or cat's paw? Do we know anything about a man called Wilkie Collins?'

'Captain Wilberforce's visitor?'

'The same. He certainly recruited a Mr Ginger Scott who described him, probably rightly, as a con-man. Porteous may have other uses for him, such as leading the pack in the search for Makepeace. I think he's worth investigation in depth.'

Lampeter acknowledged the suggestion without grace.

'It's a possibility,' he said. 'I'll get on to it. I'd be grateful, Mr Campion, if you left it to me. I know you've got friends in high places at the Yard, but I'd like to use my own contacts if you don't mind. All I need is a bit of background and last known address. Right?'

Corkran did not allow time for a reply. He swivelled his chair towards Mrs Devenish, addressing her with an underlined courtesy in his voice.

'Your contribution has been the most valuable until now. I think we should take full advantage of it and concentrate on the activities of Porteous so far as we can. Did you discover anything further about him? Restaurateurs are often very useful contacts and Guido, if I remember, is a name-dropper and a gossip.'

She accepted the compliment complacently.

'Yes, yes. I made a few inquiries on our behalf. Mr Porteous arrived in a Rolls-Royce from a car hire firm – Daltons. He stayed the night at Claridges and left this morning for Luton, where there is a charter plane airfield. No forwarding address but he has arranged for any mail to be collected. Professor Harcourt was driven back in the Rolls to Thaxted where he lives, after Porteous had been dropped at his hotel. I'm afraid that's all.'

'It may be a valuable addition,' said Corkran. 'Albert. D'you have any plans?'

The thin man rose to his feet and crossed to the window where the city spread out like a perspective map.

'The switch between the two Matthews',' he said, 'always took place at Burdon. Makepeace himself never stayed at the inn though he sometimes visited it to contact McArdie. I think McArdie, as Matthews, also had dealings with Morris Jay whilst he was there. It seems to me that Makepeace probably has his own little hideout somewhere not very far off. And putting two and two together, the number of his car, which I bet is a Rover, may be CXF 072 E, a twin to the one which was found at Brett. My own forwarding address will be the Drover's Arms for a day or two, so that I can wander around, and see what I can discover.'

He turned to Lampeter. 'By the way, I propose to tell Jay where I'm staying, just in case I can pick up another bargain. If he heads in that direction it might be tactful to leave him to me. He has a rather nervous disposition but a beautiful eye for a sucker.'

When he had gone and Mrs Devenish had vanished into her own domain Corkran lifted a detaining finger towards Lampeter, keeping him waiting for an appreciable pause before he spoke.

'You don't like him,' he said at last. 'A pity.'

Lampeter, too, took his time.

'No sir. I don't. Half the time he doesn't seem to be taking in what you're saying and yet every so often he's a jump ahead. I don't cotton to a man I wouldn't play poker with.'

17

Fisher's Catch

The Drover's Arms, it was apparent, had recovered from the loss of its mainspring and returned to a satisfactory if outwardly more casual rhythm. The West End precision of Max Newgate had been replaced by the country-gentleman-turned-hotelier touch of a new manager with a literary as well as commercial reputation to maintain. The obese menu had been reduced in size and improved in quality: cold table and cheese board burgeoned with the genuine delicacies of England.

Mr Campion noted the changes with approval and took the opportunity to discover his host's views on various rivals within easy motoring distance. The Red Lion at Great Penury was not commended, but the Blue Boar at Knightswell, the Toll House at Dudgeon and the Abbot's Arms at Market Pardon drew informed if patronizing praise.

Trailing his coat with a lack of discretion which would have surprised his intimates he paid calls upon all the suggested hostelries and several others offering less promise. The photograph he exhibited produced no conclusive result, although at Market Pardon the barmaid thought she might have served the gentleman several weeks before but she could not be sure. And his friend, come to think of it. Two old pals who sat in the corner, one whisky and water the other rum and lime, and lunched rather late. She hoped they weren't in trouble because they didn't seem the sort.

Mr Campion underlined his name and address with a tip which was not so high as to make it suspicious, assuring her that all was well. If Mr Matthews happened to call again he would be delighted to have a word with him.

Between half-past six and seven on two successive evenings he halted his car near Burdon Stone and opened the small transmitter-receiver which he had acquired from Ginger Scott, but it remained obstinately silent. At Beadles' Garage he discovered that the blue Renault which they had towed in for minor repairs had been removed by arrangement some days before. They had no address for the owner but there was thirty shillings' worth of change waiting to be collected.

The Spinster House, the best of the antique shops in Great Burdon, belonged to Morris Jay and was conducted with old world dignity, coupled with considerable acumen, by Miss Helm and Miss Fossett, retired schoolmistresses. He also supplied stock for Erasmus Hogarth, The Good Craftsman, Pewter Bros and The Merrythought, all establishments of the same persuasion.

When Mr Campion came to consider the results of two days' intensive wandering the total was not encouraging. He returned to the Drover's full of the depression which goes with unrequited drinking. In the hall the new host greeted him affably, his voice fruity as a medlar. In his opinion guests of sufficient intelligence to recognize a connoisseur and a man of good breeding were rare, but to be encouraged.

'A chit for you, my dear sir. You missed a phone call by half a head. I took the message.'

Mr Campion unfolded a sheet of paper scripted in an ornate Oxford style which would have done justice to a sonnet.

'Mr Porteous presents his compliments and would be glad if you will do him the honour of dining with him tomorrow evening at eight of the clock at Fisher's Mill which lies hard by Masonsbridge.'

'Fisher's Mill?' inquired Mr Campion. 'Am I in luck?'

His host lifted broad shoulders. 'Providing you choose carefully and someone else pays the bill. Avoid their lobster and eschew the house brandy. Their burgundies – the best of them – are good but their clarets, except for the first growths, are pretentious and indifferent. I should know, for I laid down the cellar for them two years ago and understand their clientele. If you care to give my regards to Jeremy Clinton, who runs it, he'll look after you very well. Shall I give him a tinkle to make sure?'

'Don't bother,' said Mr Campion. 'I'd like the evening to come as a delightful surprise.'

Research among the gourmet guides was revealing to the sophisticated inquirer. Those publications which carried advertisements for Fisher's Mill ('The Trout at the end of the Rainbow') spoke highly of its attractions: the more serious-minded were guarded. The old water mill had been intelligently converted and a platform had been built out over the stream where guests on summer days could take their ease and their refreshment protected by coloured awnings and parasols in a setting which could not be faulted.

Mr Campion, arriving exactly on time, approved his host's choice. Greeted with obsequious bows and smiles he found himself ushered from receptionist to *maître* and *maître* to manager, a V.I.P.'s progress that lacked nothing except a few rose petals strewn in his path. The table to which he was wafted looked down upon a flight of wooden steps to water where swans, supercilious and remote, explored a private world. He accepted the aperitif of the house with misgiving but it proved to be a simple mixture of gin and lillet with a whisper of peach bitters. Ten minutes dawdled past, orchestrated by the lapping of the water and the chatter of open-air diners.

A punt operated stylishly upstream rounded a bend hidden by willows: the single occupant moored the craft by the steps, donned a linen jacket and climbed to within a few feet of the table. Grey hair clipped close gave the craggy features the look of an athlete or a soldier used to the tropics. The eyes were deep-set under brows which had escaped the barber's attention: schoolboy amusement twinkled for a moment. He was aware that he had been recognized and was enjoying the surprise he was causing.

'Campion? Ha! You weren't expecting me but I'm here all the same. Sorry I'm late.'

The invited guest rose to his feet. 'Mr Matthews? Or should I say Francis Makepeace?'

'In one person.' He pulled out a chair, surveyed the rest of the diners like a farmer considering a cattle market, and sat down. 'Afraid I brought you here under false colours. There was an over-charming fellow on the phone at the Drover and I had the feeling that if I said my name was "Matthews" he'd have blown his top. If I'd said

"Makepeace" I risked having a pack of hounds at my heels, so I plumped for Porteous which I thought might take your fancy. Ha! He owes me a thing or two.'

His voice had a note of deliberate truculence which was mocked by underlying humour.

'Ha!' The sound was midway between a snort and a challenge. 'That fellow Porteous – a fat scoundrel they tell me. Take my advice and use a pair of tongs if you ever have dealings with him – better still, don't. Sit down, man, and have a drink.'

He signalled authoritatively to the nearest waiter. 'A Daiquiri with ice and trimmings and a refresher of whatever my guest is taking. My trip took longer than I'd calculated, or I'd have beaten you to it. I took a punt upstream for half a mile because it will be a difficult thing for anyone to follow when I go back. Chase me along one bank and I can put myself down on the other side and vanish if I feel like it.'

'And do you often feel like it?' Mr Campion was at his mildest. His host released a delighted 'Ha!' and settled himself across the table. 'A damn good question and the answer is "Yes". I mind my own personal exclusive and private business, or I try to. Too many long noses trying to insert themselves into it at the moment – too many busy fingers feeling around for my wallet. I like to keep a jump ahead.'

A canoe propelled by a boy and a girl, slim as porcelain, tied up by the punt and the pair climbed to the platform. Drinks appeared, heavy with ice and greenery.

'Chaps who elect to disappear without explanation,' ventured Mr Campion, 'are inclined to invite attention. Make a mystery and you excite every bloodhound within sniffing distance. Perhaps you've found that out?'

'The Omega pack in full cry. I suppose I'm right in thinking you're one of them? I certainly hope so.' He did not wait for an answer but drank deeply and concentrated the force of his personality into a single mischievous grin.

'Don't bother to answer. Good food here if you avoid anything fancy. Trout, steak or salmon – you can't do better. Anything mucked up with sauce is probably poisonous – take your pick.'

He brushed discussion out of his path as if it were an importunate cloud of midges. 'I suppose I like this place because I'm damn nearly a colonial. I know it's bogus, ninety per cent of it, but it's still England, the air is great, the linen's clean and the girls would drive me insane if I was ten years younger.'

He ate with gusto, mixing a salad dressing of his own which included grated chicken's liver, and was delighted to find it appreciated.

As a good host should, he allowed his guest a share of the conversation, teasing opinions and apparently unrelated rags of information from him by simple overstatements which demanded rebuttal.

'Omega,' he said abruptly when the trivia was exhausted. 'What a firm! What a monstrosity! A great cold-hearted octopus that could throttle half Europe if it felt like it – and would if there was any money in the idea. Yet when it comes to a simple little job like tracing an ex-employee they have to drag in some independent outsider like yourself to do the job for them. D'you know why?'

'Grit in the computer?' suggested Mr Campion.

Makepeace snorted. 'Ha! You can say that again and you'd not be far out. But not absolutely bang on target. It's not grit but false pride that puts the infernal thing out. Who d'you suppose feeds the facts on personnel into its bottomless stomach? A woman called Devenish, very near the top and quite intelligent as far as she goes. You may or may not know her but I can tell you something about her that nobody else understands. That woman has had a love affair with Omega for damn nearly forty years. A blind, idiotic, gibbering, infatuation. She sleeps with it every night of her life – has an orgasm every time the name is mentioned. In her eyes it can do

212

no wrong.'

He slapped the table, making the cutlery rattle.

'And if it does, it never goes on the record. Every single bloody word that could be construed as damaging is edited right out – blue-pencilled – or altered very slightly so that the point is lost.'

'The Grand Serendi affair?'

'Ha! You know about that?' Makepeace was surprised but not taken out of his stride. 'You're brighter than you look – perhaps you specialize in that sort of thing. The Serendi trouble was nothing important – a flea bite, no more. It was the little episode which went before it that mattered, as they'll discover one day. And you won't find that in their infernal mechanical memory. I'll bet there's a file on me as thick as your fist and a card punched all over the place with little holes – I'm docketed like the parts of a Bren gun. The machine knows all about me except one essential fact, a little mistake that was suppressed before it was fed into its mechanized maw. There's a new fellow doing their hush-hush security stuff, an ex-government wallah, just retired, whose brains they can pick. You must be his bright idea. Name of Corkran, officially – called Elsie behind his back, which makes him sound like a cissy, but I take it he's not. Omega don't believe in having queens working for them and old

Auntie Devenish sees to it that they disappear if they do bob up. Is he your man?'

'He's by way of being a friend,' said Mr Campion guardedly. 'Pre-war vintage and never a rude word – except perhaps in Latin.'

'Good. Couldn't be better – just what I'd hoped. You'll take him a message from me, won't you?'

'With pleasure,' said Mr Campion. 'There's been some failure in the communication system so far. Omega likes to keep tabs on its old friends.'

'Apart from the Devenish woman it hasn't got any. But let them hear this.' Makepeace straightened his back and spoke slowly, using phrases which he had evidently prepared with care. 'I want no part of Omega. They and I owe each other nothing – not one single solitary wooden nickel. If they're afraid I may go across the road and spill any of their precious projects then I'll forgive them the insult on the grounds of insanity. *Providing that I am left alone.* If they don't call off their pack of swivel-nosed ferrets I'll take the first offer which comes along, even if it's from Pan-World itself. I'm not in the market for selling secrets, but I still know a trick or two and I don't doubt I could make them look pretty silly if I gave my mind to it. Have you taken all that on board?'

'Every word of it.'

'And you'll deliver it – loud and clear?'

'Person to person,' said Mr Campion. He turned his head to survey the harlequin pageantry of the tables where imitation candles were beginning to win their battle against the evening light. 'What I don't understand,' he added mildly, 'is why you didn't say all this in the first instance. Surely it would have saved a lot of trouble?'

Makepeace gave his characteristic snort.

'A fat lot of use that would have been. They'd have been down on me like vultures or worse, trying to pick the carcass before it was dead. I'm not in the factory any longer and I intend to go my own sweet way. I'd hoped to get away with it by a simple vanishing trick, but the idea came unstuck when poor old Tom McArdie snuffed it, and left me suspended in outer space. Now I'm forced into using threats and threats don't impress unless they can be carried out. I don't care for dirty fighting and if they're wise they'll let sleeping dogs lie. This one may be old but it still has its own teeth. Do you think you can put that across?'

'I can try.'

'Good man. Pitch it to them hot and strong even if it means talking yourself out of a job. You've found me, so the show is over. You seem to have been pretty well on the ball so I hope you're collecting a packet – they can afford it. Outsiders always do well out of them when they're used. It is only when

215

you're part of the machine that they start sucking your blood as well as your brains. Ha! I remember thirty years ago when we were playing around in the Gulf there was a buddy of mine who went on leave...'

He broke off to stare across the tables, his eyes narrowed behind the untidy hedge of his brows. Mr Campion followed the direction of the scrutiny. Under the striped canopy covering the entrance to the millhouse a man was standing, glancing slowly from guest to guest.

'Face like a sheep,' said Makepeace. 'Blue shirt, grey suit and spotty bow tie. D'you know the fellow?'

Mr Campion turned his head.

'Yes,' he said. 'His name is Morris Jay.'

He twisted in his seat to make a beckoning gesture which produced a smile of wintry embarrassment from the figure in the doorway, who sidled slowly forward with the reluctant air of a man who suspected that the floor was unsafe and that a whirlpool of boiling oil rather than a millpond might lie beneath. His sallow skin had deepened to a warm ochre when he was recognized but by the time he reached the table it had become parchment, emphasizing the bruise above his right cheekbone.

He acknowledged the thin man's greeting with a formal bow but did not accept the chair which had been pushed towards him.

'I am intruding. This was not my intention.' The velvet voice was unsteady. 'I – I had expected to find you...'

'With Porteous?' suggested Campion. 'A very natural error – I made it myself. I take it you have met my host?'

Makepeace held out his hand.

'We've had dealings – never met. Bound to happen as soon as I came out of purdah. Here and now it couldn't be better. Sit down, man, sit down and stop looking like a lost soul.'

Morris Jay obeyed. Colour had flooded back into his face and he moved the chair so that he had his back to the other dining-tables. It occurred to Mr Campion that he was more frightened than surprised. Makepeace clapped his hands as if he expected to summon a saffragi to appear in place of a Cypriot waiter, insisting on hospitality before explanation.

'Ha! So you thought our friend would be dining with Porteous and wondered what the devil it was all about. I don't blame you for being nosy – I'd do it myself if I was in your shoes. The fact is I asked him here in order to cut him and Omega right out of the whole business. I've enough problems on my hands without having to dodge their squad of plain-clothes flatfeet.'

Mischievous eyes twinkled at Campion over a glass of brandy. 'No offence, my dear fellow – it's your bosses I dislike.'

Other tables were beginning to empty. A launch glowing with lanterns slid from its moorings by the steps and bustled away downstream, a bat zigzagged above the platform and vanished: the river's dank scent offered the first whisper of autumn.

Morris Jay shivered. He had not spoken for some time but whenever a waiter appeared or a party broke up he had looked over his shoulder as if he needed an excuse for keeping an eye on the door to the millhouse.

'Expecting another visitor?' inquired Mr Campion. 'We've been under observation for the last ten minutes by two characters who don't fit into the scenery. Not part of my retinue, but we're the centre of interest. If you want to vanish discreetly why not persuade Makepeace to spirit you away in his punt?'

The suggestion produced a snort of derision and a thump on the table from their host.

'Damned if I'll scuttle off with anyone until I'm good and ready. D'you know those fellows?'

The little man huddled his shoulders as if he hoped the move would make him invisible. His head bowed to avoid inquiring eyes.

'I recognize one of them. He has followed me more than once.' An involuntary twitch shook his body and he mopped beads of sweat from the dome of his forehead. 'Forgive me. I have some experience of physical violence and it terrifies me. I could not endure a repetition.'

Makepeace stood up. 'We'll see about that,' he said. 'I'll just find out what these two customers think they're up to.' He strode across the restaurant, almost unbalancing a waiter with a tray of drinks who was manoeuvring incautiously in his path, and planted himself in front of the two men leaning against the Dickensian office desk which was the headquarters of the *maître*.

From where Campion was sitting the conversation was beyond earshot but as it progressed a little of the truculence evaporated from the expressive back he was watching. Neither of the strangers was making any concession: they continued to lounge, the taller of them speaking casually, a cigarette between his lips.

Finally Makepeace indicated the distant table and its occupants with a nod which appeared to produce agreement. He made his way back to them, the glint of mischief still in his eyes.

'I asked for that one, I suppose,' he said. 'That fool at your pub, Campion, seems to have told the entire world where you were feeding – and with whom. Including Porteous himself. He's in a room upstairs and has been watching us most of the evening.

He has asked us to join him and I said yes. Ha! I rather want to meet that bastard face to face.'

18

Ultimatum

The room on the first floor of Fisher's Mill looked directly over the platform and down-stream to where the water reflected cricket-bat willows regimented against an opal sky. It was not used as a restaurant during the summer months except on occasions when there was dancing and the tables round the central floor exposed green baize tops above naked legs. Flimsy chairs were piled on a corner dais, which they shared with music stands and a shrouded piano.

A single shaded table-lamp threw a circle of light onto the one place which was occupied. Claude Porteous sat with his back to the windows, his bulk making both bench and table appear too small for their purpose. A goblet containing two fingers of spirit and a bottle of cognac stood by his hand, the only items in the picture which were sharply defined.

As the three men walked across the empty space the door closed behind them and they stood before him, each aware of being at a disadvantage. Porteous turned his head slowly, considering them in turn before he spoke.

'I take it that the stranger to me is Mr Francis Makepeace? Your reputation is for disregarding conventions, for a lack of respect for authority, for prankish trickery. When I learned that my name had been used without my consent I made a logical inference. Was I justified?'

Makepeace pulled up a chair and straddled it, his hands gripping the back.

'You're right. You've been nosing round after me for a long time and now I'm here. I don't see what you can do about it because you know damn well I don't want any part of you.'

Porteous released a wheezy sigh. He lifted a hand in a wave which included Campion and Jay.

'Be seated. Take what comfort is available. I regret your attitude, sir – I deplore it – but I hope to persuade you. You will please bear with me whilst I speak my mind and set out my intentions.'

He paused to sip the brandy. 'If you wish for refreshment I have arranged for some additional glasses which you will find on a tray by the door. We may be some time in conference.'

'The hell we will,' said Makepeace. 'There'll be no damn conference as far as I'm concerned. I came up here to tell you to go and boil yourself and to say it loud and clear. Have you got the message?'

There was no reply. Jay had moved a chair towards the table and stood behind it, hesitating. Laughter drifted up through the open window and from the kitchens somewhere below came the rattle of plates, voices shouting incomprehensible orders. Frying oil dominated the several odours cooking. Very slowly Porteous pulled a large square of orange silk from an inner pocket, crumpled it into a glowing bundle in his right hand and rested it on the table in the circle of lamplight. Presently he released his grip allowing the scarf to spring out like a flame, caught it once more and returned it to his pocket.

'We have a basis for discussion,' he said. 'Certain common interests are manifest. Be seated.'

Morris Jay alone appeared to have missed the significance of the gesture. He twisted a chair on one leg, changed his mind, and remained standing.

'I think,' he said, 'there is a point which may not have been appreciated. It seems to me a very important point, something we should not overlook. Mr Campion has no business here, he does not know what we are talking about and in my opinion we should ask him to go.'

Porteous shook his head.

'Mr Campion represents Omega and in particular a man called Corkran with whom I have some acquaintance, some small familiarity. He is an obstinate, unimaginative but tenacious individual and my intention is to convince him that I am not invading his territory. His interests – those of his firm and my own – do not coincide at any point, but he must be assured of that or we shall encounter further interference. I do not propose to discuss our project openly even here where we can be tolerably sure of freedom from eavesdroppers. Ultimately Mr Makepeace will strike a bargain with me – he has very little option – and the bargain is of no possible concern to anyone except the three of us here. Mr Campion can witness our discussion and report to his employer that Mr Makepeace is betraying no secrets and is not in alliance with any potential rival of Omega. Unless they are convinced of that they may well continue to be an interference and a nuisance.' He turned his tinted lenses towards Campion. 'I hope, sir, that you will remain and apply your intelligence to that purpose.'

Makepeace stood up and lifted the chair from between his legs holding it high and waving it slowly above the table, assessing its usefulness as a weapon.

'You're asking to get your skull bashed in,' he said. 'You'd better explain what you think you're up to before I change my mind.'

Porteous ignored the threat. He moved the lamp to one side and clasped his hands over his glass before he spoke.

'I am, as it were, in the course of drawing up a prospectus for a business arrangement which could be immensely profitable to you, to Mr Jay as the informed intermediary, and to myself. The only question which should arise is the division of the prizes and this can be satisfactorily, amicably, settled. We are all greedy men but there should be enough to satisfy even the most avaricious.

'The first, indeed the only, consideration which should arise is the bona fide – what I will call for Mr Campion's benefit the Ultimate Proof. Until Mr Makepeace produces it we cannot proceed.' He raised a plump finger. 'One further point. Mr Jay is not responsible for this suggestion in any way. Indeed, when I first mooted it to him through a third party he rejected it out of hand, and I found it necessary to take certain steps, to apply certain pressures of which he is well aware. I have gone further: I have protected his interests from spying by employees of Omega. He will be merely the honest if involuntary broker.

'But the ultimate proof is essential.' He took a mouthful from his glass and stared blankly at each man in turn.

225

'Have I made myself clear?'

'Not entirely, if you'll forgive me.' Mr Campion's mild intervention broke the tension. He had been standing beyond the immediate radius of the lamp and now drew a chair forward, sitting like Makepeace astride the flimsy seat.

'What you appear to be conveying is a threat. "Do as I say or I will attack you through Anthea Peregrine, whose scarf I have just flourished under your noses." It may of course be just a scarf of the same colour and design as hers, produced with the idea of creating alarm and despondency.' He turned to Makepeace. 'When did you last see those young conspirators?'

'Four days ago.'

'And you're happy about that?'

Makepeace was discomforted, the unease of a schoolboy caught breaking bounds.

'Good God, no. Not happy. Damn worried, in fact. I thought they might be having a rattling good time in glorious weather and with plenty of loose cash. I'd have done the same at their age. They're nothing to do with this business, so why the hell should they care? I'm not their keeper and their heads are perfectly well screwed on. If they want to spend their time rolling in the hay I wish them good luck. I'd certainly have done just that at their age.' He rounded on Porteous. 'But now I'm worried. So windy that I've a mind to squeeze your fat neck until you spit out exactly what you're up to.'

'I'm contemplating a lesson in diplomacy, in the use of reason in place of force.' The wheezy voice was soft. 'I am very adequately protected and by uncouth henchmen with no scruples about injuring elderly men. You would be most unwise to offer me personal violence. I have asked you for what I have called the ultimate proof, an expression which I am confident you understand. Without it you might be perpetrating an ingenious swindle, one quite within your capacity. When I receive it and am satisfied, we can proceed. You have two days to produce it.' He emptied his glass. 'I shall not be available in the interim. To get in touch with me you will advertise in the Personal column of *The Times* newspaper using the phrase "The iron is hot", and adding a telephone number, after which I will make my own arrangements.'

'And suppose I tell you to go to hell?'

Porteous sighed. He had picked up his stick and sat with it locked between his hands.

'It might be unfortunate, distressing to your avuncular sentiments. Young people today are so undisciplined, so uncontrolled, so unbalanced. They take drugs, become subject to illusions, drive irresponsibly. Shocking accidents, one could say self-inflicted wounds, are commonplace.'

227

Makepeace filled his lungs and expelled the breath in a long furious snort. His knuckles whitened over the chair.

'If anything happened to those kids, d'you think for one half second that anything on God's green earth would induce me to deal with you? There are plenty of others I could go to – Jay could probably name several without stopping to think. I turned you down when I first heard of you and now I see just how damn right I was. That's the way it's going to stand.'

It was some time before Porteous replied. He clasped and unclasped his hands on the ivory handle and finally raised an index finger in admonition.

'You are behaving wilfully, childishly – worse, ignorantly. You appear to have a pathological fear or a dislike for large consortiums, based on your experiences with Omega. That may be understandable. Each man has his fantasies and yours is the picture of yourself as a lone adventurer. If you reject, as you have, the conservative, the normal course, then you must perforce look to the others, to the peripheral concerns. My interests there are very diffused but, in the final analysis, comprehensive. The chances, the preponderance of the odds, is that by going elsewhere – or endeavouring to – you will be entangling yourself in the same web, but at a considerable financial loss. Middlemen, if allowed to multiply, could halve your profit and possibly cheat you out of most of what remains.'

He turned his head. 'Mr Jay, if he applies his mind, will confirm this.'

The little man had been hovering behind them in the gloom as if he was hoping to be forgotten. He did not answer. The chatter from the kitchens was abating, the throb of an electric dishwasher had taken over and on the wooden apron lights were being extinguished.

Porteous dismissed the query, his wheeze only just audible. 'The only other consideration is Mr Campion. His particular fantasy may be to see himself as an elderly knight-errant – the rescuer of maidens in distress, the righter of wrongs. I shall endeavour to clarify, to re-orientate this illusion. His efforts – if he intends any intervention – should be turned in the direction of ensuring that our transactions go smoothly. I have put certain wheels in motion, delegated certain duties, given separate and apparently unconnected instructions which only I can countermand. If any misfortune should occur to me, some shock which might impair my health or my faculties, then the consequences might prove distressing. The machine would continue to operate without its controlling mechanism.'

He straightened his back, raising his voice sharply.

'For the sake of what is termed the record –
in case you are thinking of broadcasting your
problems or seeking recourse to outside
authorities – I emphasize that I do not know
where those young people are. I have not
seen either of them since they elected, as you
tell me, to disappear and any surmise about
their future behaviour is pure speculation. I
have been out of the country for a week and
I expect to reach Paris early tomorrow morning. After that, forty-eight hours is all the
time I can allow – the limit of my tolerance.'

Makepeace had been listening with
gathering fury. He was flushed, the veins in
his temples were swelling and he began to
shout.

'Take a year if you like. Take a century. It
makes no odds to me. I wouldn't touch you
with a barge pole – you or anyone connected with you. You're wasting your breath.'
He lifted his chair again. 'Don't try the big
bully stuff on me. No one's ever got away
with that since I could stand upright. If
there's going to be any threatening around
here I'll do it myself. One more peep out of
you and I'll beat the living daylight into your
skull if I have to chase you from here to the
Grand Serendi and back. I'll smash you...'

From the gloom behind him Jay's whim-
pering appeal was lost at birth.

'Please ... please, I beg you. No violence,
no...'

The fat man faced the storm without flinching. As Makepeace halted the outburst to draw breath, he raised his stick and struck the table so sharply that the glasses rattled and a cloud of dust swam into the cone of lamp-light.

Immediately the door across the empty floor opened, a switch clicked and the whole room sprang into view. Four men were standing in the entrance.

Porteous levered himself to his feet.

'I shall be leaving now.' He turned to the men at the door. 'You two who came in the second car will see that I have five minutes' grace at least before these gentlemen depart. No doubt they have accounts to settle and they may even wish to confer over a nightcap. But the point to be observed is that I am to be free of their attentions. There will be no...'

He broke off, moving his head slowly, his eyes surveying every corner and curtain.

'I had three visitors. Where is the third?'

The men at the door returned his stare blankly. The throb of the dishwashing machine petered into silence. Voices drifted from the forecourt of the mill. 'Good night, Tony... Good night, you lot. Good night, sonny boy...'

'Mr Campion,' said Morris Jay, 'left by one of the service doors some minutes ago. It was none of my business to stop him.'

19

End of Mission

L.C. Corkran, staring resentfully over the sweltering city as it danced in ripples of hazy air, was exhibiting his ill-temper, as was his habit, by being studiously polite. An invitation to shoot the best moor in Yorkshire had fallen through, his leave was overdue and Omega was threatening one of its perennial bouts of internecine warfare. His club was closed for summer cleaning, the air conditioning of his room was not designed to introduce a breeze and his visitor had the look of a man armed with awkward questions.

'I can make time for you,' he said. 'Of course. But the process will be difficult. Forgive me if I attempt to hurry you.'

Mr Campion responded with appropriate brevity.

'The Makepeace file. From early '60 to the start of the Grand Serendi affair. Can I see it?'

'It is on my desk but not to be let out of my sight. Anything particular in mind? Most of the details I've memorized from over much study.'

'Two items,' said Mr Campion diffidently. He too was looking out of the vast picture window to where a shining helicopter was skimming over the Thames like an iridescent bubble. 'The first is his state of mind at that point. He was an angry man because of the tax battle that he'd lost. Did he blame Omega for his troubles – in any way at all?'

Corkran scowled.

'In point of fact, yes. He felt the firm ought to have supported him, brought their full weight privately against the Treasury and publicly through the lawyers if back-door pressure didn't work. He wasn't the only employee to be caught but he was the prize exhibit. He felt we let them down and being Makepeace he didn't conceal the fact. "Puking lily-gutted bloodsucking rats" was his phrase as I recall.'

'And were you?'

'It's arguable. My own view is that we should have offered some form of legal defence but if we had it would have been difficult to know where to stop – the thing might have gone right up to the Lords. *Relata refero*. The times were against such a move. For diplomatic reasons we wanted to keep the permanent officials sweet because there were far bigger considerations in the offing. We couldn't afford the little spiteful pinprick at that particular moment.' He rubbed his nose. 'You are probably unfamiliar with the

Treasury mentality, Albert. It has been my misfortune to know it unpleasantly well. I recognize Omega's behaviour, but without approval.'

'Was that the end of the story?'

'Unfortunately, no. The epilogue, so to speak, had its ludicrous side, but it exacerbated the wound. If you knew this establishment as I have come to, it wouldn't surprise you. It was typical, humourless and nearly disastrous.'

'You offered compensation,' suggested Mr Campion. 'But so little that it was insulting.'

Corkran snorted. 'You misjudge what I might call the Devenish school of thought, which is sometimes very powerful hereabouts. We had some doubts as to whether Makepeace in his particular black mood was really a reliable employee and in our customary computer-minded way we put a tame psychiatrist on to him with instructions to observe him discreetly – not with a consultation-couch routine but by apparently casual conversations in the club room we run here for senior executives, visiting firemen and so on. A scraped acquaintance leading to confidences over a drink or two – you know the form.

'Unfortunately Makepeace spotted him from a mile off – it's possible someone acted as an informer, but I doubt that – and he led the poor fellow the devil of a dance. It was only when Makepeace began to talk about his dream love-life with Mrs Devenish as the reincarnation of the Empress Theodora that he knew the game was up.' He cleared his throat. 'They were both very angry men as a result of the episode, though to do the head-shrinker justice he reported that Makepeace was perfectly normal and all that was required was a large increase in salary. Omega could have afforded it.'

'The graceful gesture,' ventured Mr Campion. 'I suppose it wasn't made? That brings me to item number two – continuity of contract. *Was* it preserved?'

Corkran dismissed the suggestion. 'Certainly. He was our senior adviser until four years ago. Up to that time he had been ours, body and soul, for thirty-five years and he still has a small retainer, which keeps him on call, in theory, and in practice prevents him from working with anyone else in our line of country. There is no question about it. Why do you ask?'

'Your men in the field retire normally at fifty-five. In the case of Makepeace he did another five years, so presumably his contract was renewed. You're sure there was no break?'

'None,' said Corkran flatly. He crossed the room to his monstrous desk, twisted the file towards him and flicked through the folios. 'Here you are. Expired '60, renewed '60 for further period of five years. Salary and emoluments greatly increased. All the figures and so on... Capital sum agreed instead of noncontributory pension to be awarded on expiry, October '65. After prolonged negotiations, copies of which are given as extracts in brief. The thing is cut and dried.'

'I wonder,' said Mr Campion mildly. 'I wonder if we could have a word with Mrs Devenish?'

Corkran lifted an eyebrow towards the clock. 'She doesn't approve of you. That fact will have the virtue of making her brief, so be sure she tells you as much of the small print as you need.'

His request brought her waddling into the room, her crocodile handbag beneath her arm, with the air of a matron asked imprudently to deal with an untidy bed.

'The Makepeace contract,' said Corkran. 'Mr Campion has a query about the five-year renewal. I take it you were right in the picture at the time?'

She sat down, her back very straight, every fibre of her woollen two-piece bristling.

'His demands were outrageous right from the start. He felt aggrieved and was trying to recover his tax losses at our expense. He behaved like a schoolboy and was very rude into the bargain.'

'But in the end,' suggested Mr Campion, 'there *was* a bargain. Did the negotiations take long?'

She pursed her lips. 'Some months. He made matters more difficult by going off and leaving no proper address. We dealt with him in a series of cables which had to be forwarded through his bank. It was a quite deliberate impertinence designed to show his independence. My own opinion was that we should have let him go but of course I never expressed it. After it was all agreed he went straight off to the Grand Serendi.'

'In October 1960?'

'He arrived at Port Bundi on the 17th, two days after the trouble, and joined the *Delta Omega* by tender, five days later.'

'The original contract,' persisted Mr Campion, 'expired in February, I think. Was the new one back-dated when it was finally straightened out?'

Mrs Devenish became suddenly defensive. Her tone was flat as if she had been offered an insult which she proposed to ignore. Deliberately she evaded the point.

'Mr Makepeace had done no work at all for us for some months. In that time he went gallivanting off and tried to hold us to ransom by making ridiculous demands. We were absurdly generous to him over the new agreement and to expect us to back-date it after his behaviour was altogether too much.'

'Did he ask you to?'

She tossed her head. 'Oh, yes. He argued

237

and threatened and was extremely abusive. We saw no reason to pay him a gratuity for protracting the negotiations and I told him so myself. I hope that answers your questions.'

Mr Campion was dejected. 'Yes,' he said. 'Yes. I'm afraid it does. It means the end of my mission as far as Omega is concerned and leaves me with a most unpleasant problem which is really none of my business.'

Corkran suddenly, uncharacteristically, exploded.

'Damn it, woman! Then there *was* a gap. For seven months he was entirely on his own – no obligations to anyone – free to do just as he pleased. And we had no possible claim on him during that time – worse, we could have established one and we turned it down.'

'We refused to be bullied,' said Mrs Devenish obstinately. 'He had to be shown that he couldn't get his own way simply by cabling idiotic demands. Some of his messages were unprintable and I suppressed them. He is an impossible man and we were quite justified in treating him as we did. We were more than generous.'

She collected her bag and stood up. 'Mr Campion seems to think that he has achieved what was asked of him. I hope that means that he knows what Makepeace is up to and that he'll have the goodness to tell us here and now.'

Mr Campion took off his glasses and

polished them. He was leaning against the ledge of the window, his legs stretched straight before him.

'I can make an informed guess,' he said at last. 'I think that in the unfortunate gap which has escaped the Omega records Makepeace went off on a geological expedition of his own. He was probably trying out a theory that he'd been brooding over for a long time. I think he has discovered a very large field of diamonds – so large that it could upset the world market.

'I think he perceived a heaven-sent opportunity to get his own back on Omega, the government and the world in general. I don't suppose that he knew anything about the diamond business but he had an old friend, McArdie, who enjoyed bargaining, buying and selling expensive items like cameras and tape-recorders. I think he got McArdie to explore the market, selling stones one at a time, the smaller ones first and in the last two years larger ones at regular intervals.

'The diamond trade is a very secret business, especially if your goods have no pedigree from De Beers, which is the almost exclusive world syndicate – ninety per cent, I believe. I am guessing here, but I think these may be very high-grade diamonds – sufficiently so to ruffle the dovecotes when they began to appear from an unknown source. I think they learned the trick of secrecy very early on – about four years ago. To cover themselves they invented Matthew James Matthews, and established him as a genuine person by using the passport and papers of a dead man.

'Both McArdie and Makepeace called themselves Matthews when it suited them but McArdie did the hard selling, either round Hatton Garden or at the Drover, which was a very convenient place for Mr Morris Jay to meet him. I think the mysterious Mr Jay deals in diamonds as well as antiques and I suspect that he operates outside the syndicate – that is, he buys under the counter from places like Liberia. He's a genuine antique dealer but I think his imported furniture sometimes is used for smuggled goods. I think the two little men who were being investigated by Lampeter when he met with his unfortunate accident – the Worth brothers – are diamond cutters working exclusively for Jay.

'I think McArdie's death caught Makepeace right on the hop. He was establishing himself very comfortably at Brett under the name of Matthews and it must have hit him right in the wind when he walked into the Drover and discovered that his *alter ego* was officially dead and that his friends had been informed about it. He couldn't re-appear claiming to be Matthews without a lot of awkward explanations and he had no intention of letting Omega know what he was up to.'

Mr Campion paused, looking at Corkran above his glasses.

'I think he's floundering now in very deep water – deeper and dirtier than he realizes. And the sharks who swim in those parts are of the large size.'

He sighed.

'And I think, regretfully, that the whole episode is nothing whatever to do with Omega.'

Mrs Devenish raised her hand to her throat so slowly that the movement protracted the silence, making the gesture mesmeric. She swayed forward as if only the weight of her sensible shoes was preventing her from falling, recovered her balance, shook her head and began to fumble blindly in her handbag. The handkerchief which she pressed to her lips emphasized the frightening pallor of her prim, unlovable face.

'Excuse me,' she said. 'I think I am ... there is not enough air in the room...'

Corkran watched her departure without attempting to be solicitous. For some time he scowled at the door. As he turned his head his expression changed by gradual degrees from ill-temper to cynicism.

'Do you remember a play by Lonsdale in the days when we were young and gay? The last line was something about being a "bloody old fool"?'

'Yes,' said Mr Campion thoughtfully. 'I do. The piece was called *Aren't We all?*'

20

The Henchman

L.C. Corkran, one eyebrow raised and the other contracted in a scowl, appeared to be concentrating his ill-temper on the dome of St Paul's as if he hoped to annihilate it by willpower. The thought which was trickling through his mind was unworthy and, he decided, probably useless. He dismissed it: one hand at work castrating facts for the record was enough. He gave thanks for his good fortune in being a late arrival on the scene.

'I suppose you're right?' he said at last. 'You must be. And we haven't a leg to stand on. But there are still points which escape me. For example, what was Porteous doing with Ewan Harcourt when the Devenish woman spotted them?'

'Picking his brains,' suggested Mr Campion. 'Trying to establish where Makepeace might have been when he made his discovery. It must be quite near the Grand Serendi. Look at the dates. He was at Port Bundi within two days of settling his contract and since it is a difficult part of the world to reach my bet is that he was there already. We know he's interested in aqualung diving. I would guess that his treasure comes from the ocean bed outside territorial waters – the shoals north of the group where there's been volcanic movement and navigation is dangerous. The "Sailors Beware" department covers a wide are in those parts.'

'Pointless speculation. I take it Makepeace has troubles of his own with Porteous? Why can't he take the whole business to De Beers and sit back to a tidy fortune?'

'Because he's an obstinate, ornery, opinionated, overgrown undergraduate with a chip on his shoulder the size of a caber and a natural taste for private enterprise and mischief. He's still the Boy Francis of forty years back. I don't want any part of his adventures. He's not safe out ... and nor is anyone within a mile of him.'

He turned to survey Corkran over his glasses. 'Elsie, I think you owe me a favour. I'd like it now.'

'Anything you care to name within reason. Our cheque by the way is going to shock you. Outside consultants are handsomely treated at this altitude. What else?'

'The result of your Mr Lampeter's researches. He was going to do some work on a man called Wilkie Collins if you remember. I'd like to see the dossier, or better still the expert himself.'

Corkran considered the request.

'I don't want him put in the picture about Makepeace at this stage. On the other hand if I tell him the inquiry is cancelled and you are no longer associated with us it may make him more cooperative.'

He was right. The news brought a controlled glint into the square man's eyes, and his mouth, which had been obstinately set as he came into the office, relaxed. With the change in status he became a senior man conferring a favour on an outsider. He expanded handsomely, speaking with the confidence of authority confirmed.

'Clifford Jermyn Collins,' he said, laying the file on the desk and opening it. 'Also called Wilkie and sometimes of course Lottie. Aged 41. Only one conviction and that's for a confidence trick – a variation on the old Ponzi share-pushing swindle. It doesn't do him justice – not representative. He's what you might call a useful all-rounder. A professional criminal with enough sense not to specialize so much that his handwriting gets known.'

'Any record of violence?' Mr Campion's query was deferential.

Lampeter checked a frown at birth: he disliked being forestalled. 'Quite a bit. My contacts say a total lack of control when he's upset or caught off-balance, and a foul temper. You're thinking, I suppose, of the man who was killed at Brett whilst he was nosing

245

around in Makepeace's bungalow? Collins might fit the bill for that job. Very likely; now I come to think of it.'

He flicked a page. 'Suspected of beating up a woman he thought was double-crossing him and marking her for the rest of her natural – knocking out a total stranger he mistook for a plainclothes man – running down the manager of a very classy West End clip-joint when he was trying to get into the protection business at a point just too high for it to work. There's a lot more: all due to hasty temper rather than calculation.'

'In the ordinary way of business you said he was a smooth operator?'

'Oh, yes. Claims to have been at Eton and Balliol when it suits him and does it convincingly. In fact, expelled from Totham at sixteen for blackmailing a housemaster. Never at Oxford except for a week-end he cadged from a don he'd scraped an acquaintance with on one of those cultural tours to the Greek islands. He sold him a non-existent gold mine. Middle-class origins, so to speak, meaning that his father was a gentleman farmer who didn't make the grade owing to a taste for whisky.'

He produced a photograph, showing a well-tailored figure, tall and patently respectable, standing in a London street, his right arm raised grasping a newspaper, evidently hailing a taxi.

'Taken two days ago. We have others, but this is the best.'

'I recognize him,' said Mr Campion mildly. 'He was with Porteous at Fisher's Mill. I took the opportunity to drift out of the encounter and study the henchmen whilst their attention was diverted. A rather tough collection, I thought.'

Lampeter skimmed the print across the desk.

'Keep it if it's any use. There's a good deal of additional stuff. He's in the money just now. He's hired several self-drive cars, mostly Mercedes, from Daltons, who charge carriage trade prices. The semi-permanent girl-friend has moved into a new flat in St John's Wood and is spending a tidy figure on her tidy figure, if you follow me.'

He paused to see if the joke had penetrated and warmed to Mr Campion's smile.

'There's a great deal of stuff here, if you'd care to run your eye over it. All recent contacts, with records if known and last addresses. A tough collection you called them and you're not far out – protection racket strong-arm men mostly. But there's one name which doesn't fit.'

Mr Campion accepted the folio, taking his time to digest the contents. When he had finished it he closed the green cover and placed it on the desk.

'You're a great loss to the Yard,' he said.

'Twice as good results and in half the time they'd need. My respectful congratulations. You said there was an odd man out there. I thought I saw two.'

Lampeter was still in expansive mood.

'So there are. One is honest as far as we know and might be called an accident of birth. The other is Edwin Lee Forsdyke trading as Milburn Associates of Dover Street.'

'It used to be called the Peerage Pop Shop when I was a boy. Have times changed?'

'Yes sir, they have. Most of the nobs sold off their jewels years ago and the business has changed hands. It's not quite so respectable now though the wall-to-wall carpeting is still just as thick, I'm told. It's still the classiest pawnshop in the business and the most discreet. But the new boss sails very close to the wind. The grape-vine says he's a fence.'

Corkran had relaxed his scowl during the discussion but now it returned at full strength. As far as Omega was concerned the sooner the inquiry was concluded the sooner the result could be consigned to oblivion, an exercise which was best performed without developments or complications.

'Take the whole wretched file,' he said. *'Palmam qui meruit ferat.* Put a plain cover on it and forget where it came from. And ask me to dine with you soon, Albert. I live just now as a guest in a wilderness masquerading as a club where the members are reputed to make their own trousers.'

'Next week, Elsie, if I survive,' said Mr Campion.

Dismissed, he left the city for the more leisurely atmosphere of the Morris Gallery in Knightsbridge and wasted long hours before he was able to reach the proprietor in person. Mr Jay, by instinct secretive, had become even more elusive as a result of his adventures. Only the possibility of a sale and the threat that it might be lost if the proprietor did not appear in person persuaded Mrs Woolf the saleswoman to bring him scurrying in a taxi from some unknown bourne.

It was nearly midnight before Mr Campion finally returned to his flat, a temporary home in an Edwardian block in Duke Street. The foyer consisted of an apparently empty porter's cubbyhole, a staircase, lift gates and an unpromising bench for luggage or visitors awaiting reception.

As he closed the outer door a girl's head appeared behind the window of the porter's box and the frame was pushed upwards. She ran her fingers through untidy hair and blinked at him solemnly, her eyes heavy with sleep.

'Hang on a minute,' she said. 'I've only just woken up. You're Mr Campion, aren't you? My name's Peregrine and I've been trying to find you all day.'

21

In Place of Valour

Mr Campion's service flat, rented on a short lease, had been furnished by the management in late Metro-Goldwyn-Mayer style, but it was comfortable and well equipped with refreshment. Miss Peregrine surveyed it with satisfaction and relaxed like a cat in the largest of the armchairs. She lay back arching her neck against the cushions, a gin and tonic in her hands. Even in crumpled jeans she made a thought-provoking picture to any masculine eye.

'Better,' she said. 'Miles better. Oncer said that you were civilized and really quite with it. I think I ought to have taken his advice and spoken to you that day at the Drover.' She sighed. 'Now I'm going to have to crawl. I hope you don't mind. If I'm not very good at it, please assume I'm grovelling. I want to grovel fantastically. I'm afraid I really do need help.'

'Are you hungry by any chance?'

She shook her head.

'Full of pub sandwiches. I've spent hours in smelly telephone boxes and got practically no joy at all. A bath would be nice but it'll have to wait. First of all…'

'First of all,' said Mr Campion, 'you're going to tell me what has been happening to you for the last day or two and just how you got away. I take it you've been a guest of Mr Porteous?'

'I was nabbed,' she said and sat upright so that she could take a sip from the glass. 'Caught in a ditch outside Great Burdon whilst I was trying to be too clever by half. A couple of louts bundled me into a car with a rug over my head. They didn't hurt me – at least not so much as I hurt them – but there wasn't a lot I could do about it, apart from kicking their shins and biting anything I could find. Since then I've been in a flat run by a tart – a sort of wardress as far as I was concerned – long pearly fingernails, dozens of wigs and expensive scent that knocked you backwards.' She began to mimic refinement superimposed on adenoidal cockney. 'Ever so chic – ever so cute. A flaming bitch who was longing to scratch my eyes out. She terrified me.'

'Any sign of a man?'

'Oh, yes. A resident jailer called "Gutsy" and a boy-friend – a rather tall city slicker type called "Cliff", as far as I could discover through my keyhole. He called her Pet.'

'That would be Master Collins, a friend of Porteous. Where was this flat?'

'I haven't the faintest. I was a bit dopey most of the time, I think, but it was high up – near the top of a big block and quite new. My window looked on to an air-shaft with a view of hundreds of loo windows and a patch of sky. Air liners cruised about most of the time. It was in London. anyway.'

'You managed to escape?'

She took another sip. 'No. This is the shame-making part of the story. I was just dumped. Early this morning when I was asleep – doped again, I think, because my mouth tastes disgusting. I was carried out of the place, a gag – a filthy dirty handkerchief – in my mouth, wrapped in blankets and things, down in a lift because I remember feeling sick and being driven off in the back of a car. It might have been miles or just in a circle – I haven't a clue.

'Then I was plonked down like a bag of rubbish, in some bushes. It didn't take me long to get free – I don't think it was meant to – and there I was in Regent's Park near the Zoo. I didn't even have to ask because it said so.'

'Very unnerving,' murmured Mr Campion. 'What did you do next?'

'There isn't much you can do in Regent's Park at half-past five in the morning. I had a pound note they hadn't discovered in my jeans so I walked for a bit – to Swiss Cottage where I got a taxi from a caff. I couldn't think of anywhere to go except to the hotel Daddy and I once stayed at when we went to town together, the Cambria, near Marble Arch. They weren't very pleased to see me and it took me hours to get breakfast. You can't go throwing your weight about when your working capital is down to about thirteen shillings and you look as scruffy as hell. I felt better after I'd hocked my watch – I got four quid and a dirty look for it, after a bit of trouble – but it restored my self-respect.' She leaned back, closed her eyes and shivered.

'That is,' she said, 'until I'd finished my telephoning. It took me two hours and six calls at three shillings each to find old Matty and another ten bob's worth to get any sense out of him. Jay was cheaper at six-pence a time but it wasn't until half-past eight this evening that I found him. Then he wasn't really what you'd call co-operative. In fact he was so horridly cagey that I began to wonder whose side he was on. But he did say one thing, which is really honestly why I'm here. He said you were fairly on the ball and I'd better ask you if I wanted a sensible answer. It's taken me the rest of the night to find you, but here I am.'

'So I see,' murmured Mr Campion. 'Hang on a minute.'

He disappeared into a room no bigger than a cupboard and emerged with coffee and biscuits.

'After this the limit of my repertoire is bacon and eggs. Did Jay or your friend Matty tell you what they were up to?'

'They damn well had to admit it because I guessed. I don't know if you were told about this but Matty got me to go to his bank and collect a little wash-leather bag from his family deed box. It was very carefully sealed and quite small and there was something in it the size of a marble or a bean. That was when the penny dropped. I didn't tell Oncer because Matty was being so secret and "X the Mystery Man" about it that I thought it would spoil his fun. He still thinks he's conducting a private war against the Dreaded Woo-Woo. Silly old goat.'

'What happened to the bag?'

'It's in a rabbit-hole in the ditch where I was picked up. I think I could find it again if pushed. In fact I know I could. I just had time to stuff it away before they grabbed me. I suppose it's stinking valuable?'

'A thousand or two, I expect,' said Mr Campion vaguely. 'Worth a search when the weather's a little calmer. Did you realize that Oncer had been caught as well?'

She frowned over the coffee.

'Oh yes. There were two cars chasing us from Burdon that night and the second one went charging off after him. The men were talking about it once they had me under control. They didn't think he'd get far.'

'You haven't seen him since?'

Anthea put down her cup, straightened her back and rose to her feet.

'No, and nobody else has either. I think that's rather serious, don't you?'

'Very, I'm afraid.'

'So do I. I couldn't get any sense into Matty's head and God knows I yackety-yacked at him for hours over the phone. He just says he'll bash the fat man's head in for him when he catches him and he has the whip-hand so Porteous had better shut up and call it a day. I used to think Matty was a spendid old pirate, keeping up with the boys, recapturing his youth and all that malarkey. Now I see he's just an obstinate old fool – the sort of silly ape who looks the facts straight in the face and walks on, slap into a brick wall or a mineshaft.'

'What about Morris Jay?'

She shrugged her shoulders.

'He sounded like a frightened mouse trying to be discreet in case the cat heard him. He's worse than useless and yellow all through. He nattered something about Porteous wanting to see what he called the ultimate proof – which doesn't mean a thing to me – and that I ought to try and persuade Matty to show it to him.'

'And did you?'

'I had another bash. I couldn't get a grain of sense into his head and we had such a row that I don't think he'll ever speak to me again. Not that it matters.'

She looked directly at her host, her eyes very large: not threatening hysteria but wide with anxiety.

'I want Oncer back,' she said deliberately. 'And I want him now. You've got to help me because as far as I can see you're the only creature in all this bloody hoo-ha with his head screwed on straight. You realize that? Do please try.'

'I hope to oblige,' murmured Mr Campion. 'You have a very persuasive manner. I think Mr Porteous appreciates it too. Almost certainly he let you go on the strength of it. I think he calculated that as soon as you knew the position you could be relied on to force your friend Matty's hand.' The suggestion was not acceptable before she had turned it over in her mind and taken two mouthfuls of coffee.

'And I've made a muck of it. What the hell can I do now?' She sat down abruptly, her hands clasped between her knees, her head bowed. Mr Campion considered an avuncular gesture but temporized by offering a cigarette, which she smoked with surprising inexperience.

'When the odds are so long that the battle really is lost,' he said at last, 'the only course is graceful surrender if you want to avoid tears. You wouldn't mind that?'

'Mind?' Miss Peregrine was contemptuous. 'I wouldn't mind if Porteous got his fat fingers on every diamond in creation. I don't want any wounded heroes or baffled master criminals or any of the dreary old stuff which was dead before I was born. I just want Oncer Smith back in one piece so that I can freeze him for myself and I'm too tired to care if I sound like a bitch. Have you got that?'

'Yes,' said Mr Campion. 'Yes, I have. I sympathize. I'm a little too old for heroics myself.'

Anthea stubbed out the cigarette, drank the last of her coffee and ran her fingers through her hair.

'Good. What's the next step? I mean, where do we wave the white flag and how do we twist Matty's arm?'

'The next step,' said Mr Campion judicially, 'is a nice long night's rest. I suppose you didn't book a room at your Cambria Hotel?'

'The money wouldn't run to it. In the mess I was in I didn't look good for a room on tick.'

Mr Campion produced a notecase but she waved it away.

'Don't worry. I've thought about this. You seem to have plenty of space and you're quite respectable. I could doss on a sofa if it won't get you into trouble.'

'The spare room is at your service.'

She relaxed for a moment.

'Good. That's settled. Now, before I pass out, how do we deal with that pig-headed old battleaxe? I'd sleep a lot easier if I thought you were capable of making him see sense.'

'I don't think I can,' said Mr Campion regretfully. 'My idea is to conduct our own private surrender and argue afterwards.' He regarded her solemnly over his glasses. 'I'm afraid I started to wave the white flag this afternoon. Tomorrow morning it will appear in *The Times* personal column. A little item for the attention of Mr Claude Porteous. It says "The iron is hot".'

22

Telephone Exchange

Miss Anthea Peregrine, the silken sleeves of a dressing-gown rolled to her elbows and the hem trailing around her bare feet, roused her host with tea and newspapers at an unconscionably early hour. She was glowing from a bath, her hair a bronze aureole still slightly damp as she rubbed it with a towel.

'We're in,' she announced, presenting a folded page. 'Right next to the crossword puzzle. "The iron is hot" and your telephone number. That's all.'

'Let us hope it doesn't attract the lunatic fringe the compulsive ringers-up who have a few minutes to spare after they've solved the last clue.'

She sat decoratively on the far corner of the bed and began to nibble a biscuit. Oncer, Mr Campion decided, was a fortunate young man and it was unlikely that any other point of view would occur to him for the rest of his life.

'I thought I might be your secretary for today and answer the phone. I'm quite good at it – holding off parents for my father when they decide to play up – all that trad stuff. I sound years old and fantastically efficient. They always assume I'm the matron.'

'You can hold the fort at least until I'm bathed and shaved. If Porteous rings don't chat with him but if he recognizes your voice it could be an advantage. I'd like him to feel that everything's going to plan. When I'm dressed and in my right mind you can go shopping. Nothing like a few new clothes to give one confidence.'

She raised her knees to her chin and clasped them, regarding him solemnly as if for the first time.

'You really are on the ball. Do you make yourself look dim as part of the act? Twenty quid would wash the smell of Chanel Five and Pet's nail varnish clear away. You can have it back as soon as I get home.'

It was a day for phone calls. Just before nine Morris Jay's mellow whisper, deepened by the instrument, came discreetly over the wire, giving the impression that he hoped he was out of earshot from unseen listeners.

'It has not been easy. You took a great risk in putting the advertisement in so soon. A day might have made all the difference, as I told you.'

'But you've got it?' Mr Campion's inquiry was so casual that he might have been discussing the purchase of a packet of cigarettes.

'Oh, yes. I have certain undesirable contacts – one often has in my business – and they were prepared to help ... for a consideration. I hope you will forgive me for going above the figure I suggested but there was no alternative – a seller's market and the commodity is comparatively rare.'

'Nobly done. Did your friends but know they're having this one on Omega Oils. No ... no more yet from the enemy. Can I find you at the Gallery when the matter is fixed?'

Jay's hesitation was prolonged.

'I suppose,' he said at last, 'I suppose I am essential? I should be very happy to be excused. My reputation is a delicate affair – very easy to damage. I could not face violence again.'

'Your presence is vital,' said Mr Campion firmly. 'It's your wisdom and authority not your strong right arm we need. I foresee an almost gentlemanly transaction and once it begins I shan't let you out of my sight.'

He rang off.

The second caller proved to be a garrulous salesman who was at least displaying enterprise on behalf of his stock, which, it finally emerged, was elaborately personalized notepaper. Anthea dealt with him coldly. Her tone was still chilly in answering the next summons but the crackling wire produced a notable change.

'Washington D.C.,' she announced. 'Yes. I

261

can take the call.' She held out the receiver. 'For you. Lady Amanda.'

The limpid voice came clearly over the line. 'Your new secretary sounds special. I hope you manage to keep her.'

'She's a temporary,' said Mr Campion. 'Just out of school.'

'Albert, are you having one of your sprees?'

'A little deputy adventuring. I seem to be dealing with an Aladdin's cave.'

'Watch out for Ali Baba.'

'I am. Is your trip successful? A necessary journey?'

'Very. Six Super Seraphims, two Morning Stars and a fleet of Cherubim Mark Nines on the order book. With any luck and a bit of wangling we can buy the villa at St Remy. Can you fix it?'

'Next week, unless I'm under arrest.'

His guest, who had vanished during the several expensive minutes of the conversation, put her head round the door.

'My wife,' he explained. 'She's been selling aeroplanes – rather well as it turns out.'

'With a voice like that she could sell central heating at the equator. D'you realize it's four o'clock in the morning in Washington just now? She must be very fond of you.'

'She is,' said Mr Campion absently. 'It's time you did your shopping.'

Just before noon there was a further sum-

mons followed by a display of business courtesy technique which had become familiar.
The synthetic accent dripped with golden
charm.

'Good morning. This is Omega Oil. Mr
Lampeter would like to speak to Mr Campion if it is convenient.'

'It is.'

The brusque approach of the man himself
was in acute contrast but the resentment
had evaporated.

'Information that might interest you, for
what it's worth. I called my people off the
inquiry yesterday but there were some I
couldn't reach until late last night. You
might like to know that Collin's girl-friend –
Mrs April Bosworth, she's on your list – has
done a flit. Fairly hurried, my chap thinks,
because she's missed an appointment with
the hairdresser whose shop is part of the
block and she hasn't cancelled her milk or
the newspaper. But lots of luggage, which
suggests the best part of her wardrobe and
the intention to make quite a stay wherever
she's going. My chap got into the flat later
on. She took her own car, which is hired, so
it's anyone's guess where she's headed.'

'When was this?'

'Fifteen thirty hours yesterday. Hope it's
of use to you. It closes the file as far as I'm
concerned.'

'I'm deeply grateful. Another grey hair but

263

it won't show amongst the rest.'

At Guido's, Mrs Devenish, lunching at her accustomed table in the corner of the balcony, had the satisfaction of cutting Mr Campion dead. It was a curiously old-fashioned gesture which she permitted herself in the way she might on another occasion have taken a cup of strong tea she had had in her mind's eye all through a busy morning. She appraised the clothes of the young woman he was escorting with complete accuracy and decided that the girl had a dress sense and an eye to value for money. The sleek blue mohair suit over a white frilled blouse was deceptively simple and could not be faulted even by a jaundiced mind. A niece perhaps: he ought to buy her a string of good pearls for her twenty-first and he could well afford to do so out of the money Omega has wasted on him. The arrival of Mrs Steinbeck provided a welcome change of subject.

During the afternoon Anthea had a lengthy if specious conversation with the caretaker of her father's house at Brett, and in her capacity as secretary took several calls for her temporary employer. Only two were significant.

'From Antwerp,' she announced and placed her hand over the mouthpiece. 'I can hear wheezing. I think it's him. Please wave the white flag like all hell.'

Her host took the receiver.

'Mr Porteous?'

'Mr Campion? I assume I am addressing you as an agent – a plenipotentiary. The inference is clear – inescapable. I have observed the newspaper message but the telephone number is not what I anticipated. Do you speak with authority?'

'I have something of interest to show you.'

'Excellent. There must also be co-operation, providing that I am satisfied. It is the first essential, indeed the only one. Are you in a position to assure me of that – to guarantee it?'

'My instructions,' said Mr Campion primly, 'are to offer no resistance at all. Upon one condition which you very well know.'

A rheumy cough came more clearly over the wire than the words which Anthea was straining her ears to catch.

'You are making an accusation, an inference, which you cannot substantiate – it is quite incapable of proof. No matter. I am not proposing to deal in quibbles, provided we understand each other. There is no reason why you should not achieve your objective within a matter of hours after we reach agreement. I shall use my good offices – my influence – to that effect. In your presence and within your hearing. There will be no question of delay or subterfuge. Do I make myself clear?'

'Beyond question.'

'Then we may proceed. I am in Antwerp, where I shall be engaged for some hours, what remains of the day. There is an aircraft here at my service which is centred on Luton, a convenient airport. My suggestion, my proposal, is that we meet at Great Burdon in the hotel with which we are all familiar, the Drover. I shall be alone, apart from a chauffeur who will take no part in the proceedings. If the matter is of interest, I shall be unarmed.'

'That makes two of us.'

'Very well, then. Mr Morris Jay's presence is required since I regard him as comparatively honest and he has an interest in the transaction which is likely to be extremely rewarding to him. The necessary documents are being prepared but you may tell your principal that if he wishes to vary them in detail I preserve an open mind. Mr Makepeace will be signing a contract which is exceptionable. You may assure him of that.'

Mr Campion's voice was deliberately colourless. 'I doubt if he will bring himself to speak to you,' he said, 'but you can take it that I am acting for him. He will agree to anything I pledge him to do but I hope you will excuse him from meeting you face to face. If you remember our last encounter perhaps that is just as well?'

Heavy breathing punctuated a long pause. 'I am opposed to violence. It is possible, conceivable, that you have a point. I mistrust men who lack self-control. You will arrive with credible authority to act on his behalf?'

Mr Campion measured his words, speaking with solemnity which was uncharacteristic.

'You have seen the man and you know his record probably as well as I do. He has a sense of schoolboy honour, a perfectly straightforward code and he will abide by it. Anything I sign he will accept without question.'

Again the line went silent: warning signals indicated that time and money were ticking past. Porteous was not to be hurried.

'A young woman's voice,' he said at last. 'A voice which I think is familiar to me, answered my call to you. May I infer that Miss Peregrine is with you?'

'You may.'

'Her influence, no doubt, has been paramount in making this agreement?'

'Exactly,' said Mr Campion. 'As you supposed. A very determined young lady. Do you wish to speak to her?'

'I shall deny myself that opportunity, that experience. Since the basis is acceptable I shall detail the practical considerations. I shall reserve a suite tomorrow at the Drover for an encounter – the Milton if it is available or the Chaucer. They are both large – commodious is the term the hotelier applies –

and self-contained. I shall arrive as near six in the evening as may be feasible in the light of traffic conditions. If you and Mr Jay arrive sooner, pray avail yourselves of the hospitality which I shall offer and make any security arrangements you may think prudent. If you intend to use the service of bodyguards you are free to do so provided our own privacy is fully respected. Miss Peregrine may be present if she chooses – it would be understandable, commendable, to want to allay any anxiety she may feel as rapidly as possible. If you have anything to add, pray propose it.'

'You seem to have thought of everything,' said Mr Campion. 'I wish I had your gift.' He rang off.

Anthea took a deep breath. 'Phew! I heard nearly all of that. You're taking a chance, aren't you, pledging old Matty's word like that? Do you know what you're up to or are you just playing it all by ear?'

'Inspiration and natural talent,' said Mr Campion modestly. 'Coupled with charm. It goes a long way, you know, when you're waving a white flag.'

The final call came just before six. Anthea, who had picked up the receiver, had no chance to respond, for the diaphragm was vibrating with distorted fury. She held it at arm's length.

'Matty,' she said. 'I had him like this

yesterday. You'll have to wait for him to cool before you can understand a word.'

Mr Campion took her advice. The tirade continued for some time with such force that the air seemed to grow heavy with an impending cloudburst.

'I am afraid we have a very bad line,' he ventured at the first lull. 'I gather that you're not entirely happy about something. Could you speak a little more slowly?'

'Happy!' The microphone resumed its ominous crackling. 'Happy! I can't imagine what the blazes you think you're up to. I've only just seen your damned piece in the paper and I'm here to tell you you're talking out of the back of your neck. Nothing would induce me to deal with that pot-bellied crook. He knows it – you know it – we all know it. He can't hold the boy indefinitely without getting into a mountain of trouble and since I've no intention of bargaining he hasn't a leg to stand on – not a snowflake's chance in hell. No point to it at all. You're an interfering jackass, a goggled nitwit, and I'll thank you to mind your own damn business.'

'Miss Peregrine doesn't agree with you.' Mr Campion sneaked the thought in during a break for breath.

'She's infatuated – not using her mind. If she wasn't besotted by that long-haired young calf she'd know that I'm absolutely right. As for Porteous, if I have one more

269

yelp out of him I'll...'

'Break every bone in his body?'

The suggestion produced a moment's pause. Makepeace returned to the attack with vibrant fury.

'I'm not being funny, so don't try to get away with it. I've never been dictated to in my life and I've had a gutful of smooth swindlers. Tell Porteous that – from me – if he gets in touch with you. Tell him to boil his head in crude oil. Tell him...'

Mr Campion put down the receiver and poured two glasses of sherry from a trolley loaded with bottles. The instrument continued to jitter like a record played too fast for a considerable time before a continuing buzz announced that the line was disengaged.

'No dice there,' said Miss Peregrine. 'I told you he was a silly old goat. Now he's crackers as well. What do we do next?'

'We finish our sherry,' said Mr Campion, 'in comparative peace, which is beneficial to the digestion. Then we decide where we're going to have dinner.'

'And tomorrow?'

'Tomorrow looks like being a busy day for one and all. Your ex-Uncle Matty appears to have withdrawn from the contest but as it turns out he is in no position to say the last word. You and I and Mr Jay are going to conduct an independent surrender.'

23

The Ultimate Proof

A fifteen-hundred-weight black van with a warning light mounted on its roof, its windows protected with heavy steel mesh, drew up at the elegant Carolean doorway of the Drover's Arms at precisely six in the evening. The single word 'Safeguard' was displayed on its flanks.

Its appearance was so incongruous that it attracted overt attention from several guests arriving to take vesper refreshment and a fat bay pony from the riding-school took exception to its sinister presence. The girl who was attempting to dismount turned to her companion.

'The Gestapo are here, Roddy. Shall I sacrifice my all to save your life?'

Two men descended from the cab whilst a third remained at the wheel. Peaked caps, black shirts and jack boots created in most onlookers a strong desire to keep at a distance.

Mr Campion approached the pair with diffidence.

'One of you should be Sergeant Bowen?'

'I am.' Six foot four of human brawn clicked heels so sharply that a Nazi salute seemed inevitable but the face beneath the shining peak was sweatily amiable. It had been a very hot day, promising to turn stormy.

'Splendid. I think you're causing a little too much of a sensation here. Perhaps you could park farther along? I'd like you to be accessible but not too obvious.'

The big man produced the friendly almost patronizing grin which goes with uncontested strength.

'Anything you say. You want the box now?'

'Not before the last of the party arrives. The rest of us are here now.'

He described Porteous in some detail. 'Give him five minutes when he appears. Then two of you will bring the box to the Milton suite – the name is on the door – and remain just outside it. No doubt we shall lock ourselves in. If Mr Porteous has a man there too it would not be surprising, but I'd prefer it if you don't fraternize. When we're finished, Mr Jay will give you any further instructions.'

The grin widened.

'Clear as a bell, sir. If we're back in town before midnight you save yourself thirty pounds in extra charges. I thought I ought to mention it.'

'With any luck,' said Mr Campion, 'the

deal will be over in less than an hour.'

He returned to the hall of the Drover and climbed the wide staircase leading to the main corridor, at the far end of which was a door bearing the word 'Milton' in gothic lettering. The suite consisted of a large low-ceilinged room whose white panelling had settled without argument into the gracious irregularities of old age. There was much oaken furniture collected with a sense of period, gay with chintz over the more comfortable chairs. A bedroom complete with a four-poster and massive clothes-press lay beyond.

Anthea turned to him as he came into the outer room. She had been standing by the window overlooking the garden, her back towards Morris Jay who was slumped over a gate-legged table, his head bowed, his fingers drumming the dark surface, every tap adding to the tension.

'All set,' said Mr Campion. 'The security men are here. Porteous, according to Luton Airport and the A.A., is due in less than ten minutes. I suggest a cooling drink to settle the nerves.'

'It would choke me.' Jay spoke without lifting his head. 'You are really taking the most appalling risk. I know I've said this before but the more I consider it the less I like it. My reputation... We can't be sure...'

He stood up, quivering like a wet dog.

'Perhaps a glass of brandy...'

Anthea shook her head. Her pallor had magnified her eyes as if they had been over-painted and her lips were colourless.

'Not for me. I thought I'd just sit in the background by the window and try to keep my trap shut. The fat man will have to take that big ladder-back chair, so I've put it facing the light. You two next to each other on this side?'

In the garden ring doves reiterated their monotonous slogan, smaller birds were in full chorus and from somewhere below the hum of voices proclaimed that the evening session at the Ostler's Bar was already well attended. Mr Campion spent some time examining a steel engraving of Milton and a mezzotint from Morland's painting of the Drover as it appeared in 1794.

In the corridor footsteps approached and retreated, betrayed by cracking boards outside the doors of Chaucer and Goldsmith, the adjoining suites.

When the door swung open it moved silently to be halted by the pile of the carpet when it had turned nearly sixty degrees.

Porteous was framed in the gap, his appearance suggesting that he had been there some time, for he was not out of breath. He looked slowly from Campion to Anthea, nodded briefly to both of them, considered Jay's averted head and walked to the door of

274

the inner room, making sure that it was empty before he planted his bulk cautiously on the one chair designed to receive him. His jowls, pale blue from a recent shave, reflected the tint of his glasses.

'I have remarked your precautions in the matter of transit outside. Very wise, commendably prudent. I shall take it that Mr Campion insisted upon such security. Mr Jay, I believe – I am informed – relies on less ostentatious methods for the protection of his stock-in-trade.'

He had been carrying a flat black leather brief-case which he opened to produce a sheaf of foolscap documents.

'May we proceed?'

'We may,' said Mr Campion. 'In about thirty seconds.'

Heavy footsteps confirmed him and his hand was outstretched to the door handle before the knock added its own authority.

The two uniformed men stood outside, the taller holding a green metal box large enough to contain a hundred cigars, demanding a signature before it was surrendered.

Behind them a third figure made no attempt to conceal his presence. Porteous's gesture of dismissal was equally open.

'On the table, I think,' said Mr Campion. 'We shall lock the door on the inside and I shall call when we're ready. Until then no one will come in or out.'

For the first time since Porteous had arrived Morris Jay raised his head. His melancholy face, pasty as dough, was glistening and his hands were still beating a tattoo as if it were the only means of keeping them controlled.

Porteous prodded the little steel safe with a forefinger.

'I am impatient,' he said. 'The condition is bad for me, my breathing deteriorates.' He ran a finger round his collar, filled his lungs and exhaled noisily. 'Open it at once, if you please.'

Jay mastered himself with the effort an athlete might exert to lift a weight beyond his normal span. He clenched and unclenched his right hand, steadied it and pulled keys on a chain from his pocket, fitting the smallest of them into a circular hole at the side of the box, turning it twice, then increasing the pressure and twisting it four times in reverse. The lid, an inch of solid steel fitting closer than a skin, opened grudgingly. Inside lay a wash-leather bag with a drawn mouth.

Before he lifted it from its foam rubber bed he spread a black square of velvet on the table as if he were about to produce something more fragile than a cobweb, more sacred than the Holy Grail. Porteous hunched over his stick, his head thrust forward. He too was sweating.

Very slowly Jay loosened the cord at the

neck of the bag and allowed the contents to drop into the palm of his hand, a glittering shape of irregular facets, larger than a duck's egg, which glowed and sparkled as if it contained the secret of life. Lights leapt winking from its several planes like a crystal firework perpetually exploding.

'Your ultimate proof,' he said.

He placed the stone tenderly in the centre of the velvet and stood back. Porteous remained hunched, his wheezing audible above the call of the birds. It was some time before he spoke almost in a whisper.

'Tell me about this. The weight. The quality. The possibilities. I am impressed – inevitably excited – disturbed. I need informed opinion.'

Jay's nervousness had evaporated. He became professional, speaking with cautious authority.

'I have examined the stone very carefully, though I was only able to see it for the first time last night. The colour is as you see, the finest white, like the stones I have handled for Mr Makepeace – a sensationally, identifiably clear white. Its weight uncut is two thousand one hundred and twelve carats – about a thousand less than the Cullinan diamond when it was first found. As to what can be made of it...'

He shrugged his shoulders, paused to fit a jeweller's lens into his right eye, picked up the object. Between his hands the facets threw rainbow colours on to walls and ceiling.

'It is impossible to say at this juncture. Basically it is part of an octahedron group – not an unusual formation. One must allow a fifty per cent loss in the cutting of large diamonds. The cleavages may be difficult but at least two very important stones could be cut from anything of this size. There are still men in the world rich enough to afford such possessions but not many. As to value, it is imponderable, quite out of my normal sphere.'

He replaced the fantasy and sat down.

'My consortium,' said Porteous, 'can deal with these questions.' He stretched out a hand and withdrew it. 'Mr Campion, can you empower me to handle the matter? You have full and unquestionable authority?'

'I have. I consulted Mr Makepeace last night. I will give it on one condition, which you very well know.'

Porteous opened the folio in front of him, brushing the statement aside.

'I shall need written authority, witnessed – fully attested – for my satisfaction and retention. You will be so good as to consider this provisional contract. It is liberal to a degree – unexceptionable. Mr Jay will assure you that the ratios offered are above normal trading rates.'

He sat back, clasping the stick between his

legs. 'Read it with diligence. If Miss Peregrine is becoming impatient she will have to control herself. Two clauses are of the utmost importance. I require the exclusive handling right of this jewel and of the field from which it came and I shall need to know, here and now, its exact situation. If there are difficulties over the location certain amendments may be necessary in the final draft.'

Mr Campion pushed back the document which had been placed in front of him and stood up.

'First things first,' he said mildly. A telephone stood on a long oak chest beside trays loaded with bottles and glasses. He picked up the instrument and placed it on the table, where a spectrum of colours dyed the base as if it had been caught in a rainbow. 'I have the precise longitude and latitude of the origin of this pretty thing. Mr Jay has checked it himself and it is written out in minute detail. I will hand it to you without question – before reading or signing the contract – just as soon as you make one call. You will order the release of Oncer Smith now.' He paused, his head inclined, looking down on the bulky figure from above his glasses. 'Then I will affix my mark. After that I'm afraid you will have to stay with us until we are assured your share of the bargain is complete.'

Porteous puffed out his cheeks.

'You mistrust me. That is not altogether

unjustified – unexpected – unnatural. I shall not repay you in like coin. On the contrary, I will accept your assurance, your given word.'

He put out his hand towards the telephone.

As he moved a latch clicked sharply and the door to the bedroom swung wide, until it rattled against a doorstop. The man who faced them with his head covered by a silk stocking had a snub-nosed gun in his hand, pointed directly at Anthea.

'Absolute silence,' he said.

He took two paces into the room, emphasizing the threat to the girl, the mongoloid face behind the veil expressionless. 'You – Jay – throw that thing out of the window. The rest of you ... *quite still.*'

For each of them the sense of affront which follows in the wake of shock produced the same effect. Perceptions heightened, making the scene appear unnaturally slow. Porteous was the first to react. He raised his head in an effort to breathe deeply. From his throat came a wheezing rattle, a pitiable choking noise more animal than human. He rocked his body backwards and forwards, fighting for air, his eyes closed, his face mottled with purple and his arms fluttering helplessly.

'The spray,' he whispered and struggled again for breath. The spray – my pocket...'

Campion, who had risen to his feet, flicked a single warning glance at Jay, a clear instruction to obey. He made a dive for the choking man, tore at his collar and ran his hands over the sagging jacket. He located the pressurized spray which is the asthmatic's life preserver and played vapour into the gaping mouth.

Jay sat motionless, his eyes glassy like a man in a trance and on the table the shimmering prism, shaken by Campion's sudden move, sprayed a new kaleidoscope over the room.

Anthea picked up the crystal mass as if it had been unwanted rubbish, and pitched it almost casually through the open window.

She did not wait to see the hands which caught the prize before it could reach the ground but rounded on the man with the gun.

'Get out.'

He backed towards the bedroom, one step at a time, feeling for the doorpost with gloved fingers extended behind him, found it and paused for a final survey. The latch clicked, a key turned.

Porteous was still struggling for air with the hopeless perseverance of a landed fish gasping for water. His spectacles had slipped from his nose and hung hooked over one ear: his eyes were unfocused and although his chest was heaving his wheeze was irregular and shallow.

'He mustn't die,' said Anthea. 'Not now. Is

he going to?'

Campion handed her the spray.

'I hope not. Keep at it.'

He turned to the outer door, unlocked it and flung it open. Outside three curious pairs of eyes stared at him in sudden alarm.

'Anything wrong?'

'We've been hi-jacked – robbed. Did anyone pass you in the passage?'

'Not a soul.'

'There's a chap with a gun nipping out by the bedroom here – probably through a communicating door – and another in the garden. There'll be a get-away car somewhere at the back. Chase them up – at least get their number.'

The taller of the uniformed figures drew himself to his full impressive height.

'No, sir,' he said. 'Sorry. Our responsibility ended when we delivered – right here at this door. After you sign for anything you're on your own. Against our rules to behave like policemen, especially with armed men. If you want the police I'll call 'em. We'd get the sack for trying to do their job.'

From behind them the third man intervened.

'Bloody gutless bastards,' he said and ran for the stairs.

'Sorry,' repeated the giant. 'We don't make the rules. Anything else we can do? The gentleman looks ill. A doctor?' Campion looked back over his shoulder.

'Yes,' he said. 'As quick as you can.'

He closed the door and returned to Anthea. She was still bending over the half-conscious figure, pressing the atomizer whenever he opened his mouth. Jay had recovered his senses. He stood by the window, peering cautiously into the garden from behind the curtains.

'They ran through the back – two of them. The man who caught it and the one who was here. He jumped and swung himself down from a branch like a monkey. What can we do? The police...'

His voice trailed away.

Mr Campion ignored him. He placed a cushion behind the head of the exhausted man in the chair, replaced the tinted glasses, and took the spray from Anthea.

'There's very little time,' he said. He bent close, speaking to Porteous. 'Did you recognize him? I think I did.'

The fat man struggled to answer, appeared to give up the effort and closed his eyes. The whisper was barely audible, as if he were speaking in a dream.

'Collins ... double-cross ... traitor ... my fault, my bad judgement – no loyalty. Dangerous ... stupid criminal. Water...'

He was very near to collapse. Mr Campion held a glass to his lips and poured a mouthful.

'Young Smith,' he persisted. 'You were going to give orders about him. Tell me the number and I'll get it for you.'

Porteous arched his back with an effort, struggling to fill his lungs. His eyes had been closed but now they half opened, showing only discoloured whites. The wheezing became louder. 'No idea where the boy is. Details were unimportant. Better ... wiser ... left to others...'

'The number,' said Mr Campion without pity. 'You must remember the number.' He stood above the flagging body, a hand gripping each shoulder. 'You must remember the number.'

Porteous seemed to have retreated into some secret stronghold of the mind. His lips moved silently and from in his chest came a long rasping rattle. Suddenly consciousness returned in an uncertain flicker and he spoke audibly.

'Be urgent. The number is O one. Six two four. Seven five...'

His head fell back, his mouth sagged open and he began to snore horribly. From the corridor came the creak of footsteps, voices raised in argument and an imperious knock.

'Wait.' Mr Campion's voice was suddenly authoritative. He turned to Anthea. 'If it's the hotel people, help me to stall them off. If it's a doctor, let him do his stuff. Don't explain...'

'But he's having a fit or something,' she protested. 'He may die and we didn't get the number.'

Mr Campion wiped his forehead with the back of his hand.

'I'm afraid I know it already,' he said. 'It's the flat you've been staying in – Wilkie Collins' hideout. The birds have flown and I don't think Oncer was ever there. Open the door now, but don't get involved. There may not be a lot of time to spare.'

24

East Vinecross

Dr Penn emerged from the bedroom door of the Milton suite, a stethoscope still hanging round his open shirt collar, his grey hair ruffled, and a medical bag in his hand. Despite the paraphernalia he looked unprofessional, a man dragged without ceremony from work in the garden. He put down the bag and surveyed his audience, his eyes resting curiously on Anthea.

'He'll do for the moment,' he said. 'Now who's in charge here? You, young lady? You're Miss Peregrine, if I recall.'

She shook her head. The new manager had been hovering in the background torn between curiosity and anxiety. If there were going to he difficulties he was determined to stifle them at birth. He stepped forward like a coach whose team had not done so well as expected.

'Technically, of course, I am. But my guest has a chauffeur who's here and some other form of helot as well. Between us we should be well able to cope. I can arrange an extra bed so that one of them can be with him all the time, if you think it necessary.'

'Shock,' observed Dr Penn dryly, 'is a serious matter with asthmatics. He'll need watching for a day or two. And further sedation. What happened to upset him?'

'Just a business deal that fell through,' said Mr Campion. 'It was disappointing for him and a trifle unexpected. You could say he had a sudden dose of bad news.'

The doctor considered the statement and found it unsatisfactory.

'The man who fetched me here – I thought at first he was a policeman – said something about robbery.'

'He did not see what happened,' said Mr Campion blandly. 'He was not in the room when the incident occurred. If anyone was a victim of theft it was I, and I'm not making a complaint just now.'

He turned to the manager who was making no attempt to conceal his relief. 'The security people and their van were on hire to me and their job is finished. They're going home just as soon as I can dismiss them. Mr Jay, whom you know as a regular visitor, has had to leave already. Miss Peregrine and I have an urgent appointment and we want to get along. I'm afraid we'll have to leave you in charge of your guest. When Mr Porteous is able to think clearly I know he'll be delighted that you handled this whole business so discreetly. Neither he nor I nor Mr Jay believe in causing any sort of trouble.'

Anthea produced an unconvincing smile. 'We're in rather a rush,' she said. 'Goodbye.'

In the corridor she took Mr Campion's hand in an impulsive squeeze. 'That was big of you. I couldn't have taken another two seconds. Apart from getting the hell out in case old Matty's cruising in the neighbourhood, what do we do next?'

'A very good question,' said Mr Campion. 'We flee in the first direction that offers, then we decide where we're going. Away is where we want to get – and fast.'

He extricated his car from the swelling ranks outside the inn and drove eastwards into the dusk where heavy clouds were threatening. By Burden Stone the sidelights of approaching traffic were beginning to twinkle: he pulled off the road and halted.

'Council of war. How tired are you?'

She considered the question for a moment.

'Tired – no. Hungry – just a bit. Frightened stiff, if you want to know. I must tell you what I'm thinking, just to get it off my chest.'

'Very wise.'

'I think it makes sense,' she said slowly. 'I've been brooding about it ever since Porteous burst or whatever he did. It's this. Poor old Oncer isn't any use to anyone any more. He's just a liability in fact. Either they'll let him go – dump him as they dumped me – or they'll get rid of him some other way, just to keep him from talking. The kidnappers I read about do pretty lousy things if they're in a hurry and there was that wretched hotelier at Coastguards who was obviously bumped off.' She turned her head away. 'Am I nuts?'

Mr Campion did not reply for some time. His own thoughts had been running on the same lines and he had reached the same conclusion. The Collins dossier made terrifying reading in the light of the evening's events.

'We could go to the police – make a nice clean complicated confession of what you and I and Matty and Porteous and Jay have been up to. Would you be happier if we did that?'

'Hopeless. It would take hours – days. And who would we talk to? That dreary oaf Appleyard down at Brett? The local people here? "Please sir, we think we ought to tell you that we happen to have been robbed of a diamond which didn't belong to us worth half a million quid, and there's more to it than that."

'I can picture the whole scene can't you? Be your age.'

'You have a point,' said Mr Campion. He twisted towards the back seat of the car and reached for a leather document case which he placed on her knees.

'I know quite a bit about Mr Wilkie Collins – the chap with the gun who outsmarted us.

He's evidently been considering double-crossing Porteous for quite a while. His plan worked pretty smoothly, so he's certainly given it a lot of thought. By now he and his chum, probably another of Porteous's misjudgements, will be well on their way to see a fence. His girlfriend, Pet, whom you encountered, is a Mrs Bosworth and she's waiting for him somewhere in the wings. We can forget her.

'The fence is a man called Edwin Lee Forsdyke who operates a very high-class pop shop in Dover Street. I don't think they'll meet there, or anywhere in town – possibly not even in England.'

He paused to zip open the case and produce a folio. 'The chances are that the negotiations will take some time. I certainly hope so. My guess is that we have about twenty-four hours before they reach boiling-point, and after that we may be in for a spot of bother.'

For the first time that day Anthea laughed.

'You're marvellously in period,' she said. 'A spot of bother – jolly poor show. Face up to it, chaps, we've still got a sporting chance.'

She turned to him, wide-eyed and angry.

'I don't see it myself. What the hell can we do?'

Mr Campion paused before switching on a dashboard light which fell directly on the papers in his hand.

'This is a list,' he said, 'of all the people who are known to be associates of Clifford Jermyn Collins, particularly people he's been in touch with lately. Most of them are pretty dubious types. Porteous used him as a general factotum for his dirty work and asked no questions.

'With two exceptions they have criminal records. One is Forsdyke, who's never been nobbled but will be, sooner or later. The other is Collins's younger brother, Gordon.'

'What about him?'

'He breeds dogs,' said Mr Campion. 'Alsatian guard dogs. German sheep dogs, if you like. Does that suggest anything to the modern mind?'

'Fatty got his dog there—'

'Very likely. It also suggests kennels, quite a bit of space for exercise – the sort of place one wouldn't visit uninvited. If I were choosing a hideout for an unwilling guest I don't think I could do better.'

Anthea whisked the folios from his hand.

'I think you're brighter than you pretend – positively incandescent. And handsome with it.' She began to read aloud. 'Williams ... Chitty ... Scott ... Downer ... where is this damn brother?'

'Bottom of the next page,' said Mr Campion. '"Gordon Lumley Collins. 'Pleydells' near East Vinecross, Snipehurst, Kent. London sixty-five miles." From where we

291

are about as much again.'

'If we drove like the clappers,' she said, 'we could be there by about one in the morning. Do you think you could make it?'

'With the aid of my mechanical wheel-chair, I might. Tell me, if Oncer was dumped, as you were, where would he head? Towards you, presumably, but where would he expect to find you?'

'He'd try ringing Matty first – where he'd get a dusty answer – then Brett. We could leave a message at the house telling him we're on our way. But' – she tossed the case over her shoulder – 'd'you know what I think?'

'I do,' said Mr Campion, 'and I agree.'

'We're wasting time. Porteous said "be urgent", remember? Get on with it – drive as fast as you like. You can't scare me.'

A splatter of rain struck the windscreen as the car purred forward, the prelude of a torrent which held them to a crawl.

'Arriving on strange territory in total dark-ness isn't my idea of good tactics,' he said. 'I think we should make a reconnaissance at first light. After that it may be just a question of barging in and making an ugly scene. It depends on how much of the story Brother Collins knows – assuming that Oncer is there.'

'I'm betting on it,' she said grimly. 'Oh, can't you go any faster?'

Mr Campion did not respond to the appeal. He drove steadily through veils of water towards the comfort of the Catherine Wheel at Henley, where civilization greeted them with cold food and an unrewarding telephone.

They ate in silence absorbed in speculations which were not to be shared. Finally Anthea emptied her glass and raised her head.

'Better now. I've got back my cool. Does your dossier thing say if that place is on the telephone?'

'It does not. You're thinking of the "fly at once – all is discovered" approach? It might work. On the other hand it might create just the sort of alarm and despondency we're anxious to avoid.'

'I was thinking,' she said, 'that no one's at their best at six o'clock in the morning, especially if they've got a guilty conscience. We could ring up from somewhere quite close – there's bound to be a box in the village – and give the impression that there're hundreds of us. After that we just sail in hoping we've made a good guess. Does that make sense?'

Mr Campion was cautious. 'After the dawn patrol we play it by ear. First, a brief sleep in town if you can manage to unwind a bit. We ought to start about four by my reckoning.'

'Say half-past three...' she broke off as a second thought occurred to her. Her smile was pure naughtiness. 'And after it's all over,' she said, 'you are going to have a hell of a lot of explaining to do, aren't you? To Matty, I mean. I don't want to sound like an ungrateful cow but when he catches up with the news...'

'We'll cross that bridge when we come to it,' said Mr Campion. 'I think we should be on our way.'

The village of Snipehurst squatted sleepily atop the first rise of land above the flat marsh country which spans the coast from Hythe to Hastings. At five in the morning it was swathed in September mist, magnifying the oasthouses into medieval castles as they loomed briefly into sight and vanished. East Vinecross, a pin-point on a large-scale map, proved more elusive. All lanes, it seemed, led to East Vinecross and none of them directly. It was a melancholy area where hop poles raised regimented heads above the dimness, interspersed with dark acres of alien pines where the Forestry Commission had done its dreadful worst.

Mr Campion's Jaguar crept cautiously through tunnels of fog where no birds sang, until progress became almost impossible. He halted the car, opened the door and stood for a minute listening. From somewhere ahead the clink of bottles in metal cages drifted through the murk.

Yard by yard he edged forward until a

gentle incline brought them unexpectedly to an area where visibility was possible at twenty paces. Sidelights glowed palely in the greyness and he drew level with a Land-Rover whose shadowy owner was loading it for a milk round.

'East Vinecross?' A cheerful voice answered Mr Campion's shout. ''Tis all East Vinecross hereabouts. Whom you wanting?'

'Pleydells.'

A metal crate and its contents clattered into the truck and a man approached, his face a vast unshaven grin.

'No distance at all. Half a mile down the lane, turn left at the fork to Kestrels, left again then right by the old barn and it's dead ahead. Notice says: "No through road". You can't miss it. Won't do you no good though.'

'Why not?'

'Nobody there. Ain't bin two days now. They'll get reported, I wouldn't wonder. You'll not get in, less you've got keys. There's wire and that. Old Army dump.'

In the clearer air the going was easier and the directions seemed simple after travelling blind. Anthea clung to the words with single-minded determination.

'The fork to Kestrels ... left ... right by the old barn.' A straight track, which had once been asphalt but was fast returning to nature, brought them to a high fence of concrete stakes and a cat's cradle of barbed wire in which was a gate with the same uncompromising protection.

A fading notice board bore the inscription:

W. D. Property
R.A.O.C. Stores (No. 6 Depot)
 Southern Command IV
All passes to be shown.

Across it in heavy white paint the words *'Pleydells – beware of dogs'* offered no welcome.

25

Dogs' Dinner

The arrival of the car was greeted by howls of animal fury which doubled and redoubled until the air reverberated with frustrated violence. Five large Alsatians roared suspicion and defiance from behind vicious barbed strands which experience had taught them to avoid, setting off an invisible chorus of rage from somewhere within twin rows of black nissen huts, rotting like gigantic woodlice, dead without burial. Their shouts were answered by taunts and threats from down the valley until the barking of dogs spread in eddies of anger away into the remoteness of the thinning mist.

The high double gate, a framework of wood covered by a mass of wire, was padlocked with a substantial chain. An examination of it produced nothing except a renewal of ear-splitting resentment. A group of milk bottles sitting in the weeds confirmed the owner's desertion.

'What now?' said Anthea. 'I don't think kindness to animals is going to help. This place gives me the "be urgent" feeling worse than ever – the purple heebie-jeebies from a standing start.'

Mr Campion sniffed the air.

'I'm going round – down wind,' he said. There may be another way in. Keep them interested – shout back if your charms begin to fade. Wave a rug at them – throw it at the gate if they show signs of following me. Then get back into the car and stay there. They may be hungry.'

On either side of the approach road lay an area of uneven ground covered with scrub, tree-stumps and lopped branches. He made a wide detour before he reached the fencing, but the enclosure was continuous and where a second entrance had once existed, nailed planks reinforced with a coil of Dannert wire barred his way.

The layout of the ex-Army dump was simple enough and there had been no attempt to change it. Inside the perimeter, to the right of the main gate, a small square blockhouse in concrete had once been the reception office and guard room. It stood at the near end of an avenue of huts, and facing them at the far end the blurred outline of a single-storey building in concrete suggested that it might be the living quarters of the present occupant. Unattractive washing still hung damply in the air and an attempt to maintain part of what had once been a regimented kitchen garden had ended in surrender to bindweed and nettles. To the left of it on an unlikely slope the remnants of goal-posts marked the site of a recreation ground.

Mr Campion made his return journey with equal circumspection. The Alsatians had abandoned their threats and suddenly he came upon the grey outline of his car looming from a patch of mist some distance from the point at which he had left it.

As he hesitated it lurched forward on the pitted track, accelerated violently and charged the gates with the force of a batter-ing ram. They cracked, resisted almost imperceptibly, collapsed over the bonnet and were swept into the enclosure. The car swerved violently, straightened only to skid again and came to a full stop a dozen yards beyond the squat concrete block.

Around it the dogs circled, snarling new threats, spurred by fright and the impu-dence of frontal attack. Mr Campion ran whilst opportunity beckoned.

He reached the lee of the guard room unnoted but the windows were boarded and the back door unyielding. Ahead of him the line of nissen huts offered cover without protection. He paused, his heart and lungs protesting at the sudden demand upon them, but no means of defence appeared.

A second dash brought him to the corner of the main concrete building and he paused again. There was glass in the windows ahead of him, set in metal frames with catches that might be lifted from within if he had time to smash one before his scent betrayed him. A dark shape moving like the wind circled a nissen hut behind him and vanished. He began to fling pebbles high above the corrugated iron curves towards those in the farther row. His third shot brought success with a clatter which was audible above the clamour. The fifth and sixth found their targets. The diversion brought renewed fury. Answering the cue, the horn of his car added its own note of confusion. He ran for the back of the main building, found an unlocked door and closed it behind him with a split second to spare before a furious yelp and the crash of paws on wood announced that he had been discovered.

The haven he had reached was a long comfortless rectangle, furnished with an army trestle table, a broken chair, a range of shelves on the far wall piled untidily with tins. Four large metal bins, two pot-bellied sacks and a collection of buckets squatted on the concrete floor. The place smelt musty, like the corn-chandlers of his childhood, and he realized that this was the preparation room for the dogs' food.

He had arrived at sanctuary by way of a paved yard. Through the window he could see that beyond it was a second enclosure fenced in by innocent wire netting in which there was an open gate. The area which once had been grass was well trodden and dirty. It contained two zinc troughs, a decapitated metal water butt and a miniature wooden gibbet from which hung a brass shell-case.

His discoverer was still sniffing and scratching at the door but fury had given way to whimpers of expectation. Mr Campion opened a window, flung out two of the largest biscuits he could find and was rewarded by a bark of pure delight.

He filled two buckets from the sacks and tins of dog food and opened the door without any suggestion of caution, carrying his load almost casually into the feeding area. About him the ex-enemy wheeled and pranced in the new ecstasy of anticipation. He struck the improvised gong with a heavy spanner which dangled from a hook in the supporting post, delivering a series of rapid blows which has a standard message for dogs and humans alike. Food is ready: come and get it.

Before he could distribute the meal into the troughs five excited and hungry customers had lost all interest in his existence and were concentrating on more important matters. This was a routine they understood. He closed the door to the open-air dining-room without arousing a single suspicious sniff.

After the tumult came a lull broken by sporadic protests from the inhabitants of the hut nearest the living quarters, diminishing complaints speaking of hope deferred.

Mr Campion walked slowly towards his car, the spanner swinging as a precaution from his right hand. The Jaguar was not a happy sight: the broken framework of the gates festooned the roof and the bonnet, two headlamps were smashed, the bumper twisted and the sleek grey nose irretrievably crumpled.

As he approached, Miss Peregrine was extracting herself without elegance from a half-open rear door. She turned to him, her face colourless, her eyes wary with apprehension, her voice small and out of control.

'Sorry about that,' she said. 'I couldn't bear it any longer. It seemed the only thing to do. I'll pay for it all – really – now at once if you like. Do you hate my guts?'

She hesitated, colour surging back until it became an undignified blush. 'That was pretty nearly the trick of the week. How did you work it?'

'Kindness to animals,' said Mr Campion briefly. 'Not your formula, if you remember, but it worked. They're away to their meal. The others will have to wait for a bit.'

Her self-possession returned, bringing anxiety in its wake.

'Is he here after all that – Oncer, I mean?

Mr Campion did not answer directly. He crossed the cracking tarmac between the two lines of huts to the opposite side, hesitating whether to turn right or left.

'Somebody is,' he said at last. 'I flung a handful of stones at these monsters by way of creating a diversion. It seemed to me that apart from the dogs somebody answered back. Listen.'

They waited in silence for a full minute but the only sound was a melancholy wail echoed without enthusiasm from the same hut.

Anthea strode away down the line.

'We can't open them all,' she shouted, 'it would take hours. The one with the strongest padlock first. This one – no, this.' She began to run.

He followed her at his own pace, stopping at the side of each hut, striking the corrugated iron and waiting until the resounding clangs were still, listening for an answer which did not come.

Anthea reappeared at his elbow.

'The second from the far end,' she said. 'Lots of the others aren't locked. One of them hasn't even got an end wall – my car's in it, just parked there. It proves he's here. He must be. Oh, do hurry.'

The padlock was new and the staples which it united had been driven firmly into timber strong enough to resist attack despite peeling paint. Mr Campion, using his spanner as a lever, was nearing exhaustion before the wood split along the grain, cracked from the doorpost and flung him off balance. He staggered backwards, dishevelled, giddy, grimly aware of his age and reached for his spectacles to wipe away the film of condensation which made them useless. Anthea had vanished.

He found her at the far end of the hut kneeling beside a body lying face downwards on a divan bed covered with rags which had once been army blankets. A hand trailed on the floor gripping a shoe and the tousled head was buried in a bolster stained with iron mould.

'Oncer,' she whispered. 'Oncer. You oaf ... you flaming nitwit ... are you all right?'

Mr Campion bent over the limp figure and turned him gently on his back, raising the shoulders and pulling the bolster forward. For an intolerable moment the head lolled flaccid and uncontrolled before the current of life began to flow.

Oncer Smith opened his eyes, blinked at blurred faces as if they were part of a dream and shook himself into consciousness.

'Heard you knock,' he muttered. 'Very loud ... very clear. I was asleep ... tried to bang back.' Suddenly his voice strengthened. 'Don't try that damned flat beer. I think it's doped. Been sleeping for days ... still sleepy.'

His eyelids drooped and he yawned luxuriously, nestling against Anthea's shoulder.

'Better when I've had a shave,' he said. 'Good night.'

26

Property on Loan

Breakfast at Pleydells, a protracted and sporadic meal, consisted of an assortment of unlikely items. Anthea, storming excitedly through the untidy kitchen of the main building, located coffee, tinned anchovies, beer, pressed beef, butter, mustard pickles, potato crisps and rusks. She laid each new discovery on the table, nibbled a sample and fled back to the hut where Oncer was lying.

Mr Campion took stock of the situation. The house had been occupied and made comfortable, if not luxurious, by a man and a woman who had packed hurriedly and left in a car whose tracks he had no difficulty in identifying. The telephone had been disconnected expertly, the wires unscrewed so that they could be easily replaced. Haste but not panic had been the order of the day.

The remaining inhabitants, two bitches and eight half-grown puppies who occupied roughly constructed kennels in one of the huts, were temporarily pacified by the appearance of food and he turned his mind to the problem of transport. His own car was unserviceable. He examined it regretfully and decided that a month would be needed before it could be restored to natal beauty.

The little blue Renault sat demurely in an open-ended nissen, muddy but apparently unharmed. A search revealed the key hanging from a nail among a dozen others on a board in the kitchen originally designed to display Army orders, still bearing the inscription 76 H.Q. (Supply) Coy. R.A.O.C.

He started the engine and ran it for some moments, listening for warning murmurs which did not emerge. Anthea appeared beside him whilst he was checking the oil. She had softened perceptibly: the shadows had vanished from her eyes and her cheeks were bright. A smudge across her nose suggested some recent contact with a dusty object.

'He's fine,' she said. 'Dopey ... a bit gormless, but no bones broken. Struggling to the surface and asking for food. What do you think? Beer? Beef and biscuits?'

'More coffee,' suggested Mr Campion. 'Just as strong as you can make it. And try eggs, there are some at the back of the larder.'

Despite refreshment Oncer's main interest had not changed. He walked uncertainly between them to the living-quarters in search of hot water and a shave, finally appearing at the door of the bedroom unsteady but triumphant.

'I found some clean socks and a shirt,' he

announced. 'Too big for me but they'll do very nicely. I'm as good as new.' He sat down heavily. 'My main instinct is to get the hell out of here.'

'Back to Brett,' said Anthea. 'Forthwith – now.' Her self-assurance had returned with the recovery of Oncer but now it ebbed sharply. She lifted herself on to the table, gripping the edge with both hands and avoiding Mr Campion's eye.

'A bit of a mess,' she said. 'That's what we're in. I've told Oncer what happened, so he's in the picture. How long do you think we've got before old Matty discovers what we've been up to? Then all hell will break loose. Jay is certain to tell him – probably has already.'

'I doubt it,' said Mr Campion. 'Playing around with a human time bomb, which is what your Uncle Matthew is at the moment, is probably not his idea of fun. Mr Morris Jay is all for the quiet life. My bet is that he'll be over the hills and far away until further notice.'

'That leaves you to face the explosion,' said Anthea. 'And I have a feeling that a few kind words of apology aren't going to be much good. It's a fantastic mess I've got you into – your car smashed and a raving nut-case out for your blood. What the hell can I do?'

'You can drive me down to Brett,' said Mr

Campion. 'I'm going to stay at the Mainsail for a day or two. When does the new term start?'

'Today week. Father comes back on Sunday. That gives us two days of peace before we start explaining.'

Autumn had delayed its arrival at the mouth of the Brett river. A few elms were flecked with tarnish but the playing-fields of the school had kept a lush green and the summer yachtsmen were still revelling in the golden days. Mr Campion had to content himself with an attic in the annexe of the inn, lacking the studied elegance of the Drover but offering compensation by way of a view over the little anchorage which lifted the heart from dawn to dusk.

He dined alone, observing his fellow guests blandly from behind his glasses. There were no familiar figures and inquiries showed that those visitors whose presence had excited gossip for a fortnight past had withdrawn leaving the mystery of their stay unsolved.

The death of Max Newgate had ceased to be a wonder after the passing of seven days. After all, as Mrs Fellows the voice of authority at the Mainsail pointed out, he had been a stranger and probably up to no good. As like as not he'd fallen into the water by accident when he'd had a drop too much. People who messed around in boats without knowing quite what they were doing often

308

got into trouble that way. If Mrs Fellows had said it once, she'd said it a thousand times, but to no avail. As for the car he'd arrived in, there might be twenty explanations for its discovery off Brett Ness. The company at the bar, who had given considerable thought to the problem, favoured the theory that long-haired London wastrels wandering about the place with girls no better than tramps were responsible. Or it could be the water-skiers, a very suspect lot. Superintendent Apple-yard might have other ideas but he'd come round to their way of thinking in the end. Having had the misfortune to be born in Norwich, it was only to be expected that he would be slow, but the conclusion was inevitable.

The results of the Regatta were far more interesting because every single prophecy and bet had gone wrong. This summer, it seemed, one couldn't even rely on the wind to blow in a decent Christian fashion. The government had much to answer for.

Before closing time Mr Campion took the road to the school, skirting the grounds until he reached the track leading to Coast-guards. The cottage was deserted, the win-dows shuttered and the weeds untrodden. At least a week had passed, he decided, since there had been a visitor.

The day had finally faded, leaving the sky a million pinpoints made of detailed outlines, as sharp as if they had been cut in black paper with Victorian scissors. He walked slowly towards the bell tent, the long shed and the mounds of earth which marked the excavation of the Roman ship. Off shore the mooring light of the *Samuel Pepys* barge was reflected in silk-smooth water, and about her the masts of lesser craft made perpendiculars sharp as ebony knitting-needles. The pictures he thought, had probably changed very little in the course of sixteen centuries.

The tarpaulins which covered the imprint of the ship in the excavation had been bought second-hand from a railway which had ceased to exist, their origin proclaimed incongruously in large white lettering: L.N.E.R. (E. Sect.).

For a long time he leaned over a rail listening to the lap of the incoming tide, watching and waiting. The interruption when it came surprised him because the grass had absorbed the sound of footsteps and he had not expected an approach from that quarter.

Anthea and Oncer were standing beside him. She took his arm and spoke in a whisper. 'We thought it might be you but we weren't sure. Have you spotted it?'

'The light in the shed?' said Mr Campion. 'Yes. Someone went in there about a quarter of an hour ago. Someone with a key who arrived in a rowboat. Someone who pulled all the blinds and is now using a torch instead of turning on the light. One of your resident experts?'

Oncer shook his head.

'Old King goes to bed at ten sharp. Set your watch by him.'

'A late worker gone back to finish a job?'

'They're kicked out at six, when he locks up.'

'I think,' said Mr Campion, 'that we ought to investigate.' He turned to the shadowy figures at his side. 'But not in haste. There's only one door. If I go in, you will wait outside. If the argument gets ugly make a noise as if you were there in strength.' They moved with elaborate stealth, reaching the shed without a false step. Outside a window Anthea raised herself on tiptoe, peering into the darkness.

Mr Campion waited by the door for them to rejoin him, his ears alert.

A sound from inside the shed made the precautions ridiculous, a thud followed by the clatter of breaking pottery falling on wood and being swept aside.

He flung open the door, fumbled for the switch and found it just as a second crash made the stale air sick with impending trouble.

Francis Makepeace stood behind the long table, a length of piping in one hand, a torch in the other. The stronger light made him blink uncertainly as if he did not recognize the intruder.

Before him lay the lower parts of two amphorae which had been hanging from the central beam, fragments amongst eddying dust, whilst the upper halves continued to dangle like broken egg shells. His body was shaking, surprise struggling with anger for mastery, chased by hysteria, and for a moment he was as helpless as a child escaping from a nightmare.

Mr Campion took the piping from his hand. A single perfect amphora still hung from the roof and he twisted it gently to read the round paper label stuck to the side.

'This is the one you're looking for,' he said. 'Your own property. You should wear glasses. Your sight isn't as good as it was.'

He broke off the tapered base with a single blow.

27

Heel Tap

The lower quarter of the two-handled amphora, an inverted cone of pottery about seven inches in height, broke cleanly from the main urn to drop with a thump onto the table. A single irregular triangle of terracotta fell away from the mass, exposing white plaster of paris which filled the whole base and held it together. In the warm unventilated air, dust caught in the unshaded lamplight hung like smoke.

Makepeace seemed unaware that Campion had struck the blow which he had intended. He stared at the broken segment for some time before he shook himself violently, seized the cone and thrust it forward like a chalice, cupped in both hands, his face knotted with anger.

'My property. You said it yourself. I lent it and now I'm taking it back. You mind your own damn business.'

Anthea's voice came coolly from the doorway. She was sure of her ground when dealing with over-excited schoolboys and spoke in the soothing tone of authority establish-

313

ing order in chaos.

'Of course it's yours, Matty. Wouldn't it have been easier to pick it up in daylight? No one could stop you.'

Makepeace glowered, his anger increasing as he realized that Oncer was standing behind her. He looked slowly from one face to the other and returned to glare at Anthea.

'Ha! So your boyfriend's with you. I said you were screaming before you were hurt, as any fool could have told you. You haven't the guts of a louse – any of you. The only thing that frightens *me* is your goddam' stupidity.' He rounded on Campion. 'As for this gig-lamped jackass, if he's been monkeying around I'll make him wish he'd never seen daylight. I've just come from Burdon where they told me some cock-and-bull story about a robbery. Porteous was there and Jay had been. One of them is half dead and the other has scuttled into outer space. You two were with them yesterday so you must know what happened. If you were using my property as bait and you've...'

'Don't you think,' said Mr Campion soothingly, 'that it would be a good idea to find out if your special property isn't just where you left it originally? As you say, it would save screaming before being hurt.'

Makepeace opened his mouth to retort, changed his mind and picked the iron pip-ing from the table.

314

'That's just what I'm going to do.'

He held the base of the ampulla in his left hand, the plaster surface uppermost and tapped it sharply several times as if he were breaking up a slab of toffee in an old-fashioned sweet-shop.

It broke into a dozen pieces, leaving a glistening stone of several facets half exposed in a casing of white gypsum. He peered at it from different angles, moving it to catch the light from the unshaded overhead bulbs. Suddenly his anger vanished: he threw back his head and laughed. It was an Olympian gust, irresistible, uncontrollable, filling the shed with infectious euphoria.

'There all the time!' he shouted. 'Safe as a bug in a rug. And all of us making goddam' fools of ourselves.'

He perched on the edge of the table, tossed the treasure into the air, caught it and began to prise pieces of plaster from the shining surfaces, flicking them casually about the room.

'Campion, you should take a chunk of this wrapping back to Omega – give it to Mrs Devenish. It's as near as she'll ever get to the fortune she lost for them by being the meanest, stupidest bitch God ever put breath into. Give a lump to fat Porteous if he's still alive. And another to—'

Anthea halted him in full flight. 'Shut up, Matty, you ape – you lower fourth specimen.

315

Play it cool for once in your life.' She turned to Campion. 'If this really is a diamond, what were you and Jay playing around with at Burdon? It looked better than this thing – worth a million.'

He was mildly discomforted, taking time before he answered.

'A most superior substitute,' he said at last. 'If we were going to have a white flag it had to be done convincingly. I never said it was a diamond – I simply treated it with rather ostentatious respect. So did Mr Jay, who's particular about his reputation as an authority.'

'But not the real thing – just a fake and you never told me?' Anthea's voice had a trace of chill in it.

'A piece of very high-class rock crystal, if the truth must be told,' said Mr Campion humbly. 'It has a long technical name which escapes me just now, and it was not easy to come by. Mr Jay himself had some difficulty in getting hold of it, because he is a cautious man with more scruples than some of those on the fringe of his acquaintance. This particular example has been used more than once by a well-known practitioner in crime to deceive none-too-honest suckers who believed in buying castles in Spain at cut prices. The last owner had it in mind to repeat the trick and poor Mr Jay had to use a lot of pressure to strike a bargain with him.

'You could call it the best gold-plated brick in the business – it would take an expert to declare it wasn't genuine. Mr Porteous, contrariwise, knows all about the business side of the diamond trade but he's no judge of the commodity itself. He relied, if you remember, on Mr Jay who was very cagey about what he said. Considering how frightened he was I think he behaved nobly.

'As for me, I promised Porteous I would tell him the exact latitude where it was found, which in fact is a gravel pit in Surrey, and offered to sign on Mr Makepeace's behalf for any rights he might claim for similar discoveries made there. Perhaps I stretched a point, but it didn't occur to me to inquire too closely. I felt I could count on his agreement in principle, especially as the place belongs to a firm of contractors in Sevenoaks.'

Oncer, who had his arm round Anthea's unresisting shoulder, whistled a wolf-call.

'You had a nerve. You must have laid the bull on pretty thick.'

'A simple but convincing show,' said Mr Campion. 'The setting – the presentation – cost more than the stone. It was essential to blind him with science. I'm afraid Mr Wilkie Collins and his friends are in for a packet of trouble for their intervention in the exercise. The people he was thinking of doing business with don't take kindly to the idea that someone is trying to swindle them. They have very strict views on dishonesty.'

'I don't want to call you an unfeeling show-off,' said Anthea slowly, 'but the thought does cross my mind. You held out on me. I think you ought to have come clean.'

Mr Campion sighed. He was polishing his spectacles, making the process elaborate.

'I wanted to end it all tidily before there were any explanations,' he said. 'I wanted that thing on the table right out of the way before it caused any more trouble. I didn't want any attention drawn to the place where I thought it might be hidden. As it is, I'm going to have to give Mr Makepeace my lecture on the virtues of orthodoxy, reinforced with as much gentlemanly blackmail as seems necessary to convince him. I intend to do it right here in this very uncomfortable shed. It may take some time because I hope to persuade him to come back to town with me to find an old-fashioned uncompromising safe deposit.'

He held out his hand.

'Bless you, my children. Have a nice long day tomorrow.'

The publishers hope that this book has given you enjoyable reading. Large Print Books are especially designed to be as easy to see and hold as possible. If you wish a complete list of our books please ask at your local library or write directly to:

Magna Large Print Books
Magna House, Long Preston,
Skipton, North Yorkshire.
BD23 4ND